Julian Sturgis

Dick's Wandering

Volume 2

Julian Sturgis

Dick's Wandering
Volume 2

ISBN/EAN: 9783337195120

Printed in Europe, USA, Canada, Australia, Japan

Cover: Foto ©Andreas Hilbeck / pixelio.de

More available books at **www.hansebooks.com**

DICK'S WANDERING

DICK'S WANDERING

BY

JULIAN STURGIS

AUTHOR OF

'LITTLE COMEDIES'
'AN ACCOMPLISHED GENTLEMAN'
'JOHN-A-DREAMS'

IN THREE VOLUMES

VOL. II.

WILLIAM BLACKWOOD AND SONS
EDINBURGH AND LONDON
MDCCCLXXXII

II.

(Continued.)

VOL. II.

A

DICK'S WANDERING.

CHAPTER XIX.

DICK did not trouble himself about his cousin's startling intelligence. As soon as he could think of it, he dismissed it as an impudent fiction. He laughed and pro- mised himself vengeance at their next meeting; and then his thoughts went back again to his mother and to the subject of their next talk. Surely this was the oppor- tunity, for which he had been wishing. All the people had gone away, and his mother was alone in the house. And yet, when he had done laughing at Ossie's ab-

surdity, he still lingered before the front
door, while his face became more and more
grave; and when at last he did go in, he
went no farther than the hall. He made
less noise than usual in taking his stick
from the stand; and he lost no time in
coming out again and starting for a walk
by a path, which could not be seen from
his mother's window. He walked like one
who fulfils a duty; and all the way he kept
telling himself that his mother could not
possibly be grieved by his determination,
that she could not help seeing that he was
right. It was impossible that she should
make a fuss about so very small a matter.
He had no plan of parting with the property—nor with any part of it, save Emmens'
tiny garden. He had no present intention
of trying any experiment, even the smallest,
with the land. His farms were held on
leases which would not expire for some
years; his tenants were prosperous; his

rents were paid without complaint; he
had great faith in his agent; and there
was no eye like his mother's for the condition of the labourers' cottages. If he were
to go away for six months or a year—and
the thought had occurred to him once or
twice that possibly he might find it well
to go away for a time—the machine would
go on equally well without him. All that
he was going to do was to execute a formal
little deed, which by changing him from a
tenant in tail to a tenant in fee-simple
would make him a landowner indeed; which
would give him power to do with his land
at any time that which was for the best interest of all who lived on it—himself, his farmers, and his labourers. Dick had long ago
emphatically declared to himself that he
could not bear to limit his own freedom by
new settlements; that it would be unbearable
to see some day how a great benefit might be
done to his people, and to know that by his

own act he had made it impossible. Thus like a generous young monarch but newly come to his kingdom did Mr Hartland think of the worthy country folk, among whom he had lived as a child; thus did he regard them with care almost paternal, and with a full sense of the responsibilities inseparable from his high position.

When Dick was at home again, he allowed himself no time for hesitation. He ran up-stairs and knocked at the door of his mother's sitting-room. She was wrapped in a soft tea-gown of nun-like simplicity; and her son, as he came into the room, thought with a sudden tenderness how slight and delicate she looked. There was a look of expectation, almost of fear, in her eyes, as she looked up at him. For a moment he was tempted to put off the words, which—as he knew well in spite of all the conclusive arguments which he had lavished on himself—would cause her deep distress.

The next minute he had made the necessary effort, and begun to speak. He stood looking out of the window, and he tried to tell her of his next visit to his lawyer and of the formal deed which he was going to execute, as he had told her a thousand times of some small plan for the morrow. When he had finished, he still looked out of the window, but he saw nothing; he was intent on listening, and it seemed strangely long before he heard her words. When she spoke, she spoke very quietly; but there was something in her tone, which sent a shock to his heart.

"Are you going to sell the place?" she asked.

"No, no," cried Dick wheeling round from the window, "I'm not going to do anything with the place; everything is to be as it is; I only want to be able to do what it may be right to do some day—to keep the power."

"To keep the power!" she repeated bitterly. Though she spoke bitterly, her first great fear was gone. She was so far relieved, that she could find further relief in speech. The feeling of ill-usage, which had hurt her so long, which had been shown so seldom and never expressed save in some slight hint or polite refusal to interfere, found words at last—words which half frightened her by their vehemence. "You have never considered me," she said. "Perhaps there is no reason why you should consider me, or ask my advice, or even tell me what you are planning; but I did think—I did hope that you would consider the wishes of your father, who is dead. He always looked forward—when you were a baby, he looked forward to the time, when you would resettle the land as every Hartland had settled it before: and when he was gone,—I tried to study, that I might know what he wished; and be able to tell you; and you never cared to ask; and now I have nothing to tell you except.. that you are doing what he—what your father——"

"But mother," said Dick, for something stopped her speech, "mother, don't you see that I am going to do nothing with the place. I only want to keep myself free, till I know better."

"And do you think that you will know better than your father, and your grandfather, and all who have gone before? yes, that's just what you do think; you have always thought that you knew best about everything. It was the same at school; you made up your mind to leave; you thought that, mere child as you were, you were a better judge than your mother, and your uncle Hervie, and John Kirby, and your tutor, and everybody; you have always been like that, always self-willed and—I don't want to blame you; I know

that people have always liked you and
flattered you, and made you think yourself
a great man and——"

"No, mother," said Dick. He was
amazed and shocked. He could not bear
to hear her speak like this. He had always
admired her for her dignity and simplicity,
her self-control and calm. She had been
to him, long before he had thought about
it, his standard of perfect ladyhood, by
which he measured other women. Now
she seemed to him for the first time to
be speaking wildly; he was shocked and
almost frightened. Once or twice there
flashed across him the uncomfortable idea,
with which Betty's engagement had inspired him, that perhaps he did not understand women. It was an idea by no means
pleasant to Dick; for he was apt to con-
gratulate himself on understanding people
so easily. If one half of mankind were
really so hard to read, it might not be so

easy a matter after all to direct his course through life.

Presently Mrs Hartland spoke again, and spoke more quietly. "You are going to do nothing at present?" she said with her eyes turned from him.

"Nothing whatever," he answered. "I want everything to be exactly as it has been; everything is going on capitally. I do so hope, mother, that you will make no difference; that you will go on managing everything which you have managed before—the house, and the cottages and everything."

"Mrs Emmens, the cobbler's wife, said something to me—something which I did not understand—about your kindness——"

"Oh, I forgot," cried Dick; "I told Nicholas Emmens that I would give him his garden."

"That you would *give* it to him?"

"Yes; it's nothing you know; and you

know what he's made of it; it's wonderful;
I wanted to give it him partly for that, and
partly to see what's the most that can possibly be made with a spade out of a patch,
when it's a man's own." He spoke quickly
and as carelessly as he could, but he watched
his mother anxiously. She was still looking away from him, as she said, "I thought
that you were going to do nothing. Isn't
it early to begin giving away the land?"

"The land! Mother! A little slip of
a garden!" Dick looked at her with eyes
bright and eager. He wished so much to
persuade, and as usual he could not help
hoping that he should succeed. He had no
conception of the depth of the wound which
he longed to heal. He did not know how
long she had nursed in silence the feeling
of ill-treatment; how she had been injured
by his premature independence; how she
had cherished the annoyance, which her
self-willed boy caused, as loyalty to her

dear husband, who was dead. Now as she sat silent in her chair and would not meet the anxious eyes of her son, the feeling of personal injury was being swallowed in a rising tide of sorrow for the future of this headstrong boy. It seemed sad indeed that he should have lost the father, who would have been the best guide and guardian in the world; and whose authority, she felt sure, would never have been questioned. Of that at least she was certain; as she was certain that the man, who had been taken from her, was the wisest and strongest of men.

"I wish I could do something for you," said Dick at last, and he came a little nearer.

"Thank you; I want nothing," she said. "I think we had better say no more at present," she added after a minute.

Then Dick knew that he had better go. He stooped to kiss her on the forehead, but she did not seem to notice his kiss. She was sitting with her busy hands dropped idly in her lap. He stopped a minute at the door, half hoping that she would call him back; and then he went out, less happy than he had ever been in his life before.

CHAPTER XX.

WHEN Dick had done that which seemed
good in his eyes, and had made himself
master of his broad acres, with power to sell
them or to leave them to whom he would,
he began to think that for the present at
least there was nothing more for him to do.
No farmer demanded a new gate; no la-
bourer's cottage incurred the rebuke of the
Sanitary Inspector. Though he had full
power over his own timber, he found that
his trees were neither too many nor too
few, and that they were all in the best condition. He almost regretted that his agent
had done his work so well. He went back
to his pamphlets; and he invested in large

blue - books, which reported the fertility of land under every kind of tenure. He had no difficulty in persuading Fabian Deane to pay him long visits, and to share his studies. When he was not shut up in his den, he made himself busy in the open air. He tramped through turnips after partridges; or he took long walks through lanes and field-paths of the valley, and out over the open downs. He made expeditions in search of a horse, till he found a worthy companion for the old hunter, who had succeeded the well-loved pony of his boyhood. So with a week's covert-shooting in November, for which the house was almost as full as in August; with a day or two in each week with the hounds; with walking with or without a gun; with much study and with long thoughts, Dick's autumn and winter wore away. It was a very peaceful time. The days seemed to pass, as the days of former years. Almost

every day the mother and son were under
the same roof; and every morning and
evening· they kissed each other, as they
had kissed each other every morning and
evening since Dick was a baby.

And yet, though this mother and son
had neither quarrel nor dispute during all
those months, both were conscious of some
unhappy influence which kept them apart.
Indeed Sophie Hartland could scarcely forget for a moment that she was aggrieved.
She did her daily round of little duties
with even more scrupulous regularity than
before; but she carried to the drawing-
rooms of her county neighbours, and to the
cottages of her friends in the village, a
constant sense of injury. She was patient
and gentle as ever. She sought no sympathy and made no complaint; but the
pride, which kept her silent, brought her
but little comfort. She was sore at heart,
and the sight of the being, whom she loved

best in the world, gave her more pain than
pleasure. She was so much alone, that she
had time enough to go round and round the
weary circle of sad thoughts; to convince
herself every day anew how ill she had been
treated; and to preach to herself, till she
found some cold comfort in an enthusiasm
almost religious, that her duty to her dear
dead husband made it impossible for her to
forgive her self-willed son. She told herself again and again that she would spare
no pains to help Dick; that she would not
attempt to oppose him any more; that she
would make his home as pleasant as possible, till he had made up his mind to sell
it, or had brought home some other woman
to reign over it. Mrs Hartland's imagination was often busy with this lady of
the future; though she had faced the fact
that of course he would not consult her,
nor indeed anybody else, when he chose a
wife. She thought that he would probably

be taken in by some flattering woman; but, come well come ill of his choice, she was determined that she would yield her place in the household without a struggle. She would only pray that her successor might make her boy happy.

Meanwhile, in spite of Mrs Hartland's conscientious efforts to make his home pleasant, Dick did not find it very lively. Alone with his mother he felt a new constraint which was hard to bear. He caught himself imagining her unspoken criticisms, when he found her eyes resting on him; and he called himself a fool for yielding to such fancies. He even caught himself weighing his words before he spoke to her. The old frankness of their everyday life was lost. Dick was uneasy in an atmosphere charged with possible misunderstandings. He felt as if the silence of the house drove him to self-examination; and of self - examination he soon had more than enough. It was an

occupation for which he had no natural
taste. So more and more, as the winter
passed away, he buried himself in his den ;
and, when he had had enough of reading,
he found uncritical companions in his gun
or his horse.   When he had tramped afoot
for hours, his step would be light, and his
mind busy with many plans for the future.
When he was galloping over the grass with
a strong horse under him and the hounds
not far away, conscious of a whole field of
neighbours and friends, all riding the same
way with rivalry and good-fellowship, he
felt in full measure his boyish delight in
quick movement and the strife of comrades.
At such times, if a thought of his mother
crossed his mind, the shadow that had come
between them seemed almost nothing. A
little while, and all would be well. She
could not long be cold to him, who meant
so well, and who was so fond of her. Besides nobody had ever been cold to him for

long. Yet when he went home, there was
the shadow still; there was the same sense
of uneasiness, which it was as hard to explain as to explain away.

Slowly the winter departed, and the
first signs of spring were seen in the land.
Spring came, and with spring came Venus
with all the Nymphs and Graces, for Betty
Langdon was going to be married. All the
long winter John Torington had chafed, for
the most part silently, at the delay; and at
last the lady had consented with amiability
to be married before Lent. It was for this
wedding only that Dick Hartland had
waited; for in Dick, as in so many men
since the days of Geoffrey Chaucer, the
first breath of spring had awakened the
desire to go a journey. Once eager to go
he found no lack of reasons. All winter he
had been at home with nothing to do; and
he was tired of doing nothing. And then
to his own heart he said that, when he came

back after an absence, he would find again
the mother, whom he had almost worshipped
as a child. Always hopeful he was sure
that a little separation would do a world of
good; and that there would be no shadow of
disagreement in the future between himself
and her, whom he should always love best
of women. Mrs Hartland seemed to approve
the plan; at least she refrained from any
hint of opposition. The second person, to
whom Dick spoke on the subject was Fabian
Deane; and on that enthusiast the proposal
that he should travel again with his some-
time pupil produced a remarkable effect.
Several interests, which were smouldering
in Fabian at the moment, rushed together
into one blaze. He had been lashing himself with accounts of the persecution of
Jews in Russia and Roumania. He had
made the acquaintance of a political prophet,
who was calmly awaiting the return of the
chosen people to Jerusalem. He had been

reading as part of his study of the land
question some glowing—perhaps too glowing accounts of the fertility of the soil of
Palestine. When Dick spoke of travel,
Fabian was straightway on fire for Jerusalem, and for the plain of Esdraelon standing
thick with corn. Dick, though he laughed at
his friend's uncontrolled ardour, was quick
to catch a portion of his enthusiasm. This
journey could not but be interesting, and
the mode of life delightful. Moreover he
had had no glimpse of anything Eastern;
and he thought that he owed it to himself
to form some idea of the East. Every morning he had been studying in his paper the
last aspect of the Eastern Question. Who
could tell what the final outcome of this
latest struggle of Russian and Turk would
be? Who could tell what would happen to
Palestine, if the Ottoman Empire fell to
pieces? Was there a happier future for the
Holy Land? Was it to be again a Land of

Promise? Such questions were exciting.
There could scarcely be a better time for
the visit of inquiring youth. So everything
was in readiness before Miss Langdon's
wedding-day. The travellers had engaged
a dragoman who was to meet them at Alexandria; and all things necessary for the
journey were to await them at Jappha.

John Torington and Betty Langdon were
married under the happiest auspices. Hervie Langdon's house by the river held
plenty of people; for he was fond of adding
pleasant rooms as ideas came to him, and
had made the low-roofed irregular cottage,
while it preserved its modest air, large
enough for many friends. And now the
house was full of friends. More friends,
and acquaintance too, came to the ceremony
from London; but, though more women
than men were attracted by a spectacle so
interesting to the sex, of all the women
there was not one so lovely as the bride.

Feminine criticism could find no fault with her appearance, except that she displayed too much composure. Indeed she was more blooming than ever; and she moved her father to some show of enthusiasm by her quiet determination to have enough breakfast before she went away. And when at last they went away, they went under a smiling sky. The sun shone in the soft blue, while on the low distant hills the shadows of light floating clouds passed quickly; the wind was westerly; it was an April day which had come before its time. In the meadows by the river the grass was already rich and deep; and farther from the bank in a slight hollow of the upland field the first slender daffodils were astir. On such a day the carter jolting down a country lane tries to whistle a tune; and on such a day the hearts of young lovers newly wed should have been full of hope and trust in the bounty of the unknown years.

Dick was ready enough to feel the new life in the air. The desire of motion came from the moving stream. The river seemed to have awakened to caprice and joy. Its full dull progress under a sullen sky had changed to play of sun and shadow, and whispers in the reeds. The old river seemed young again, and in its journey down found time to linger where the sun was warm, and to lift the lily leaves in every little bay and still back-water. Dick could never see the Thames without longing to be on it. As soon as the young couple departed, and when the rest of the people had begun to wander aimlessly through the house and lawn and shrubberies, Dick went in search of Ossie; and having found him he straightway took possession of him, and of his boat. Somewhat to his surprise the perplexing youth followed him without protest. This too-ready acquiescence of Ossie excited, as it always did, a vague disquiet

in his cousin. Dick looked narrowly at
Ossie, who looked remarkably well, and
innocent. Mr Osbert Langdon had spent
a pleasant autumn and winter. He had
visited some of the most agreeable country-
houses, and had been more or less spoiled
in all of them. More lately he had been
riding with his usual happy recklessness
the best horses of a generous, but injudi-
cious, friend. Having had, as he himself
expressed it, as many crumplers as he cared
about, he had come home to see the last of
his sister before her marriage. During all
this time he had given no report of himself
to Dick; and Dick with his happy hope-
fulness had inferred from his silence that
he was not in any scrape particularly bad.
Now however he felt somewhat less easy.
When he had sculled a little way up-stream,
he suddenly stopped and fixing his eyes on
Ossie, who was lounging in the stern and
playing with the rudder-lines, he asked,

"Have you been up to anything particular?"

"No," said Ossie, but he spoke rather doubtfully.

"You are in some scrape again," said Dick.

"Dickie my dear," said Ossie with his fingers trifling with the stream, "I'm thinking of giving you a treat. Suppose I go with you to-morrow—to Jericho—or wherever it is."

"What have you been doing?" asked Dick.

"Nothing. Really and truly I don't think there's anything."

"What is it?"

"Well, if there is anything—it's this business of me and Sukey."

"What have you been doing? And who on earth is Sukey?"

"Don't be affected, Dickie," said his cousin with apparent severity: "do you mean to say that you haven't heard about

Susan Bond and me? Everybody's talking about it," he added beaming with a sweet pleasure.

"Do you mean to say that there was really anything in that nonsense? You are not engaged to Miss Bond?"

"I don't know," said Ossie.

Dick regarded his cousin with a perplexed expression; he wondered, as he had often wondered, what on earth he should do with him. Of course he should like of all things to take him abroad; but this wish made him more careful not to decide in a hurry. He began to scull again; he had a theory that he thought more clearly, when he was doing something vigorous with his muscles. However, when he stopped, he had thought of nothing better to say than,—"You don't know if you are engaged or not?"

Ossie shook his head pathetically; he seemed to regard himself as the victim of a cruel fate.

"Does she know that you want to go away?" asked Dick presently.

"It was she who told me to," said Ossie.

"Then I suppose that, if there was an engagement—it's the most absurd thing I ever heard of in my life—anyway she has broken it off?"

"I don't know. She's the cleverest girl I know; and,"—Ossie smiled seraphically as he added,—"she's awfully fond of me!"

"And are you fond of her?" asked Dick, as if he would bring this wayward creature to the point.

"I don't know," answered Ossie; and then as he saw a look of impatience on his cousin's face, he made haste to add, "Of course I like her; she amuses me awfully; and she never bores one, don't you know."

Dick regarded his cousin with a look of wonder. He could not think of anything else to say. He turned the boat and allowed her to float down-stream, while he sat with his knees drawn up, and thought. Presently he straightened his back and legs, and with a few strong strokes brought the light boat to the side of the sloping lawn. "Now," said he, "you jump out, and go and ask your father, what he thinks about your going with Fabian and me to-morrow."

"I hate Fabian Deane," said Ossie inconsequently as he slowly got out of the boat.

"You'll have to learn to like him," said Dick.

Ossie lingered on the bank and stared at his cousin. "Don't you think, Dickie," he said persuasively after a few minutes; "don't you think that you could put it better to the padre? And I'll go and talk it over with your mother. I like talking things over with your mother."

He stood smiling tenderly on his cousin, who at last began to laugh in spite of himself, and so felt obliged to say, "All right."

When Hervie Langdon heard what his nephew had to say, he looked a little rueful. "What shall I do without a child in the house?" he asked.

"Well," said Dick, "I suppose he is too much of a child to take care of a wife."

"To take care! My dear boy, he isn't capable of being taken care of."

"Then do let him come," said Dick; "there's nothing I should like better in the world."

"So be it. That's a clever girl; too clever to be in a hurry. Upon my word it is vastly amusing. Ossie!" And with his boy's name Hervie Langdon burst into one of his explosions of laughter. When the laughter was subsiding, he said,—"Take him with you. Tell me what his share will be, and I will give you the money; I don't suppose he has got any. It will be a reprieve for the dear boy anyway."

CHAPTER XXI.

WEDDINGS are generally exciting to women; and the wedding of her sister's only girl could not but be exciting to Sophie Hartland. When she had given the last kiss to Betty and had whispered a blessing in her ear, she had gone to her room for rest and solitude; and there she had been discovered by Ossie eager to tell her everything about himself. Ossie never denied himself the luxury of female sympathy; and there was no woman, not even Miss Bond, to whom he liked so well to pour out confidences, as to his aunt Sophie. Sophie listening patiently thought with tenderness of this dear boy; of his sister who had just taken the

most solemn step in a woman's life ; and of
their mother, who would have liked so well
to have listened to her boy and girl that
day. But though she thought of these dear
people, and even while she was giving her
nephew the best advice, she was thinking
far more of her own son and of his going
from her on the morrow. She was glad
that Ossie was to go too; and she made
him promise to write to her, thus cunningly
securing a second series of reports of Dick's
welfare. She knew that Dick would write
when he could; but she had made up her
mind not to be importunate about letters.
She was determined that he should have no
cause to blame her for want of consideration.
Perhaps, while she showed consideration for
his convenience, she did not realise how
much she gave to her own pride. She had
no hesitation in strictly charging Ossie to
write whenever he could, whether he liked
it or not.

At last the wedding-day was done. When it was gone—with its irregular hours, its vacant restlessness, its gaiety a little forced, with its old trappings of ribbons and laces, smiles and good wishes, cake, rice and slippers—Mrs Hartland found that, though night was come, she could not sleep. She was tired, but could not rest. She was hot in spite of the cool air from the passing river. She got up and went to the window. The quiet of the night seemed to soothe her; and, when she felt cool, she wrapped a soft dressing-gown about her, and laid herself on the sofa. Still she could not sleep. She could not help thinking, and all her thoughts were of Dick. Somehow in the night she seemed less sure of herself, less confident that she was wholly right. Vague misgivings forced her to insist again and again on the grounds of her displeasure; and yet she was tired of this insistence; she longed to rest. How wretched it all

was! Why was her only boy so self-
willed, so wanting in consideration for her
—no, not for her; she thought that she
could easily forgive that; but why had he
so little consideration for the father, who
could never claim his just authority? So
to Mrs Hartland, who was accustomed to
sleep so well, did a sleepless night bring the
recurrence of dreary thoughts. When it
seemed impossible that she should sleep at
all, she went to the window again, threw it
wide open, and leaned into the coolness of
the night. There as she leaned, a new
thought came to her, which filled her for a
moment with self-reproach, though it came
as a relief to breaking the old circle of
thoughts. She wondered, as she had wondered so often at the end of her schoolboy's
holidays, if Dick had everything which he
ought to take with him on his journey.
She blamed herself for not having considered
this question before. And yet had she not

deliberately made up her mind not to interfere in his plans in any way? She
applauded herself for having been so true
to her determination. She might hope for
the best, and pray for the best; but he must
go his own way, and be his own master.
He had chosen to decide everything for
himself; and of course she did not dispute
his right so to do. And yet it would be
dreadful, if he were ill, and had not the
proper remedies. The thought struck her
with an awful chill; she turned away from
the window. If this thing happened, she
knew that she would blame herself for
ever; that all her fine reasons for non-inter-
ference would not save her a single pang.
It was so likely too that he was going without those proper remedies. It was so like
a man to plunge into these dreadful Eastern
countries without even quinine. Then she
remembered that she had some quinine in
the small medicine - chest, without which

she went nowhere. She was too restless to sleep; she felt better if she walked about; for a time she walked backwards and forwards in the room. Presently for the sake of change she opened the door; the passage was dark and silent; she walked out very softly. As she passed the room where Dick was sleeping, she made no pause; but she listened and could hear no sound; she noticed too that no light shone beneath the door. She thought that he must be sleeping soundly. She went back to her own room; she lighted a candle and began to look over her things with a careless air. With the same careless air she noted the contents of her medicine-chest. The glass bottle, which she took out of its wooden case, was quite full of quinine; it seemed a coincidence that none of it had been used. Presently she was standing by Dick's door; she was very reluctant to go in; she thought that she was weak, and that she would be

sorry for her weakness in the morning.
And yet to put some quinine on her son's
table could be no breach of her determination; she need not ask him to take it; she
need say nothing about it; he might take
it or leave it, as he chose. She turned
the handle noiselessly; she almost held her
breath as she heard the soft regular breathing of the sleeping boy; it seemed to her
that the beating of her heart was loud
enough to wake him. With an effort to
be calm she walked very quietly into the
room. There on the floor was Dick's
weather-worn portmanteau strapped tight
and ready for the journey, and by its side
his black bag stood open; she had to step
carefully by them that she might place the
quinine on his dressing-table. That was all
she meant to do; and yet she lingered a
little. She stood still a moment looking
down at the strapped portmanteau. Then
shading the light with her hand she went

noiselessly to the bedside. Dick was sleeping soundly. As she looked at him, a sudden sob shook her; she was frightened, but he did not stir. This was her only child. Indeed he looked most childlike as he slept. The lips, which had seemed of late years so resolute, smiling often but always unyielding, were parted now; the hair was all ruffled and the cheek flushed. It was the face of her baby boy, which the mother saw. She remembered how she had held him up with pride to his father on that morning, when he rode away in the sunlight for the last time. With that memory in her heart she bent down and kissed her boy's cheek, but very softly, that she might not wake him. Then she turned away; but, as she went, she stooped for a moment to stroke the old portmanteau, which was to go with him. Half smiling at her folly, yet on the brink of tears, she hurried to her room. When she had locked her door behind her, she felt safe; there was no need now for self-restraint; she lay down on her bed, turned her face to the pillow, and cried. Then as she wept, her heart found comfort; she was glad of this which she had done; sweet rest came as the tears flowed from her; and at last she slept.

The next morning at breakfast Sophie Hartland looked cool and neat as usual; and she poured out tea for Hervie Langdon and his guests, as if she had no thought more solemn than the just distribution of tea. Everybody seemed in the best humour. The serious business, which had brought them together, had been happily disposed of; their wedding garments were up-stairs; they had leisure to enjoy this brief saluta-tion of spring weather, the sunlight on the river and the shadow on the lawn. Dick was quiet and thoughtful; but his eyes were bright with the prospect of quick

movement, with the hope of adventure. As
for Ossie the suddenness of his determination intoxicated him. In a few hours he
had collected all sorts of things for his
journey; and among the rest he had bor-
rowed from his father, and in defiance of
Dick's protest, a big revolver, which he insisted on packing in his unwarlike portmanteau. Early in the morning he was
flitting about the house; and while he
flitted about, and even later when he sat
at breakfast, he could not keep from laughing, for his heart was light. It seemed to
him that troubles ceased to be, when one
ran away from them; besides, to run away
and leave your friends agape with amazement was capital fun.

All the party were on the steps to say
good-bye to the two cousins. They divided
the interest between them; for Fabian
Deane was to join them in London.

"Good-bye, mother," said Dick; "thanks

for the quinine ; it was so good of you to
think of it ; good-bye."

" Good-bye," she said, and she kissed
him in rather a stately manner. She was
in the midst of people who knew nothing
of her conflicting feelings ; she was chilled
by their light talk and jesting, their holiday humour. When Ossie was already in
the cart, Dick turned to kiss his mother
once more. She received his kiss gracious-
ly. " I hope you will have a pleasant
journey," she said.

" Have you got the slipper ready to
throw ? " cried Ossie from the cart.

As the two boys were carried out of
sight, Sophie Hartland was waving her
handkerchief with the rest.

III.

CHAPTER XXII.

DICK HARTLAND sat in the door of his tent, which was pitched for the night on the high plateau above Sinjil in Palestine. It was midnight, and there was no moon; but in the heaven so far and deep and clear shone an innumerable company of stars. There was no sound except when a mule or horse moved restlessly, or farther off an Arab driver was crooning a monotonous song. Both Osbert Langdon and Fabian Deane were sound asleep; the latter in the smaller tent close by; the former in the larger tent, at the door of which Dick Hartland sat like a Turk, with his rug doubled under him.

Dick was unusually solemn. It seemed
as if for the first time he was under the
strange influence of the East. During their
few days in Africa he had travelled, as he
had travelled often before. He had observed
a thousand things, and all sorts of strange
people, after that first boat-load of divers
types and brilliant colours, which had come
rowing to them off Alexandria. He had
paid a flying visit to Cairo by rail; and he
had found there the most modern of Boule-
vards cheek by jowl with the changeless
Bazar. He had scrambled up a Pyramid,
as if it were no more than Primrose Hill;
and had laughed before the sightless face
of the Sphynx at Ossie's petulant criticism.
The travellers had had no time to linger;
their dragoman urged them on like the
most Western of couriers; he declared that
the right season for Palestine was passing.
Hurrying with laughter and quick glances
they had been as far as possible from the

ancient spirit of repose, which broods over the unchanging East.

Now however these young men had been journeying for many days through a land, which seemed to have seen but few new things, since Abraham pitched his tent in the borders. Indeed they might well have fancied that Abraham himself was dwelling in one of those dark flat skin-covered tents of wandering Arabs, which they had seen one day low in a long wrinkle of the crumbling hills. It was a land without roads—almost, as it seemed, without people. In the quiet days and vast still nights the friends had fallen more and more into an unusual silence. Even their sojourn in Jerusalem had not broken the charm. They had pitched their camp beside the city, and had wandered about its walls ; they had sat for hours on a house-top gazing idly across the valley at the Mount of Olives. They had wondered at the beauty of the Mosque,

which with light dome and cool clean tiles
sits, like a fair frail woman, in the place of
the gorgeous majestic temple of King Solo-
mon. They had seen what sights there
were; but even sight-seeing was a different
thing in that strange place, where the very
Jews are poor and do not care to work.
And now it seemed a long time since they
had looked their last on Jerusalem. They
had forgotten to count the days; but day
after day they had ridden slowly forward, silent for the most part, silent
and solemn as Arab horsemen. Perhaps
the air of solemnity was wholly due to
Fabian Deane. Perhaps the silence of
Osbert Langdon was due to nothing more
than an agreeable laziness; for Ossie was
apt to grow sleepy under a hot sun, and
was at times a little bored by the monotony
of this uneventful life. He was thinking
for the most part how hot it was; how
pleasant their dinner in the cool evening

would be; that a great many people must by this time have come back to London. Meanwhile Fabian was so full of burning thoughts—of humanity, of the race, of himself—that he had no time to speak; and Dick looking at him would occasionally wonder when the storm would break, when the flood would burst the dam.

The land, through which they had been riding, was a thirsty land. The low parched hills were furrowed with dry channels, where living waters used to run. There was sand and rock and scrub; and all would have been desolate indeed, had not the wild flowers thronged wherever they could push their way, spreading wide carpets in the wilderness. There were familiar flowers abundant, as tulips, marigold, and cyclamen, with many others rare and strange—in all a great and glorious company, like the stars of their Syrian heaven. But now the travellers had come up out of these dry places. Before nightfall they had passed along an old bridle-path, once a water-course, with orange-trees and fig-trees on either hand. From the plateau, where their camp was pitched, they had seen beyond the little white-walled village low rolling hills, which seemed more green ; and beyond these hills they knew that a broader valley stood thick with growing corn.

Dick sitting cross-legged in the entrance of his tent was full of grave thoughts. It was so rare a thing for him to be wakeful, when he had once laid himself down to sleep, that he was in a mood to receive a double portion of the influence of that wonderful night. The little troubles and vain ambitions of his fellows seemed to belong to another world—a world in which he too had skipped about with a full sense of his own importance. The little events of the last summer seemed to belong to some distant past, which like an oriental sage he now

might contemplate unmoved. Not only
did the dancing and dining, the light woo-
ing and rash gaming, seem petty beyond
belief. Scarcely less petty too seemed those
things political, which had been so important—the party tactics—the choppings and
changes of complicated laws, which with
much groaning of ancient machinery are
adapted, if somewhat clumsily withal, to
those changes of society, which in our
loftier moments we name, " The Progress of
Humanity." Somehow on that night to
Dick in his unusual mood the life of man
seemed something greater and deeper than
all progresses, however excellent—than all
experimental efforts to improve the condi-
tions of life. This earth was small among
the watching stars; and perhaps man had
no stronger claim to greatness than this
discovery that his earth was small—no surer
proof of something divine within him than
this power to look upward and gaze with

awe and comprehension on vast worlds
and the spaces between. Matched with
the mind of a man, who is great enough to
measure his own insignificance, the death of
a man seems no great matter. Surely this
power of imagination, of conception, of love,
cannot be nothing, because the limbs are
still. Even to Dick Hartland strong in
body and of a cheerful heart, happy in life
and keenly interested in the things of the
world, the unaccustomed thought of death
brought on that night no depression. He
felt very peaceful; he was equal to either
fate; he was ready to live, or to die if
need were.

It was natural enough that Dick Hartland, possessed as he was by a strange
solemnity, should begin to think after a
while of his mother, and to think of her
with unusual tenderness. Love seemed so
great a matter on that night, that it almost
seemed to him as if he ought to have put

aside all his plans, rather than have hurt his
mother. Such plans seemed little enough;
and after all he had made no plans, but had
only secured for himself the power of making them. For the sake of this poor power
of making philanthropic experiments, he
had hurt the best woman in the world.
She was still the first woman in the world
to him, if he could no longer believe that
she was always right. He thought of the
time when he was a little boy, before it had
ever occurred to him that she might be mistaken. He was almost sorry that he had
ever outgrown his childish faith in her in-
fallibility. These views of his seemed there
and then to be but petty things to keep
loving hearts apart. Why should he seek
to be wiser than his father? There in the
quiet of the Holy Land age after age had
passed away, and brought no change. The
past was ever present; and the wisdom of
the fathers was enough for the children.

To this boy born to the hurry, and quickened by the practical questions of the day, it had scarcely seemed strange on that night, had he looked from the door of his tent and seen the angels of God walking shadowy in the starlight. Perhaps they would come to him, and bid him arise and go to his mother. He was sure that, if he could not recover his childlike faith in her judgment, he would let her wishes influence his purpose with a double power in the time to come. Since he had left home, he had kept all her letters. Indeed he had made this a sort of small atonement, of which she knew nothing. They were pleasant letters, in which not only was no old controversy renewed, but not even a hint of any difference was admitted. They were full of news which he was glad to know, of the welfare of his friends, the prospects of the farmers, the little affairs of the village. Holding her last letter in his hand he smiled a little

at the thought that he held there a charm
against evil. Nor was he far wrong. Had
not her whole life been such a charm for
him ? To the high ideal of this little lady,
to her exquisite refinement, to the purity of
her thoughts, her son owed in great measure his chivalrous feeling for women. That
he could not seek to injure a woman ; that
he had always shrunk with a healthy an-
tipathy from · low pleasures; these facts
were in great part due to lessons learned
by a child, not knowing that he learned,
to breathing air made pure by the daily
beauty of a good mother's life. It was well
that she was the first woman in the world
to him. His thoughts wandered a little
further; and he began to wonder if she
would always be the first. Being in a
tender mood he began to consider, as he
had considered more than once in the past
few years, what sort of woman he should
marry. He had plenty of theories of what

a wife should be; and sitting idly there
he went through them once again. He
had made up his mind long ago that
when he had found his proper work in
the world, he would marry,—and not till
then. Then as his life was to be full of
activity, his wife must be quiet and gentle; with her he should find repose in the
intervals of the struggle. Of course she
would be very good, for he had no taste
for any but very good women. She must
be full of love and consideration for his
mother. He often doubted if it would not
be wise to leave the choice of his future
wife entirely to his mother. To give her a
daughter, loving and obedient, would be a
fine atonement for his own independence.
And so, after all, these vain imaginings had
for the most part tended to show that his
mother would be always the first woman in
the world to him. Even now on this night in
Palestine his first thought of his future wife

was as of a delightful gift for his mother. Then he enumerated once again all those merits and those quiet feminine virtues, which were to complete his own active life. The picture was the same; and yet at that strange hour it could not but be different. The excellent housewife of his dreams was softened by some shade of mystery; some wonder of womanhood seemed to veil the image from critical eyes; and it was with a heart filled with a deeper emotion, that he bent his head backward to gaze into the immeasurable heaven.

CHAPTER XXIII.

From waking dreams and thoughts unusual
Dick was suddenly aroused by an appearance, which seemed to bring upon him suddenly all that was most modern in this
modern world. He turned with a shock to
everyday life ; for there was Ossie coming
forth from the tent, with his blanket wrapped around him and a camp-stool dragged
behind him.

"What are you doing out here ?" asked
Ossie.

"Thinking," said Dick ; " I couldn't sleep
—for a wonder."

"And I can't sleep either," said Ossie,
who had been slumbering for hours like an

infant. "I don't think I often sleep now," he added pathetically as he placed himself beside his cousin.

"Do you lie awake for sighing purposes?" asked Dick with a levity, which seemed to Mr Langdon ill-timed.

"It's all very well for you," he said with much dignity; "I only hope you may never have to go through what I have gone through." As he struck a match and raised it to the cigarette in his mouth, Dick looked at him critically, and seeing the very comfortable expression of his face began to laugh.

"I don't believe you ever cared tuppence about her," he said.

Ossie blew a ring of smoke, and a sigh to follow. Then he took the cigarette from his lips, and observed with manifest satisfaction,—"Poor Susan! She was uncommon fond of me."

"I hope she'll get over it."

"Very likely," said Ossie pathetically;

"very likely. I daresay it would be better. It isn't everybody who could get on well with me. I don't think people understand me. You never understood me, Dick. You can't understand this business of mine. You've no sentiment."

He appeared to derive some comfort from this consideration; he wrapped himself, misunderstood as he was, more warmly in his blanket; he sighed plaintively, and so relapsed into silence. Soon however he began to be annoyed, because his cousin did not talk to him. He fidgeted a little on his stool, and then asked Dick what he had been thinking about before he joined him.

"Lots of things," said Dick; "principally death."

"Ugh!" said Ossie.

"It's just as well to think about it sometimes. Suppose you had to face it."

"I should run," said Ossie—"like a hare."

"Oh no you wouldn't," said Dick; "you can be plucky enough; I call you rather a reckless chap; look at the way you ride sometimes."

"That's all excitement. I should be ·in an awful funk, if I had time to be."

"Well then," said Dick with his inquisitorial manner, "suppose you had to choose in cold blood between dying and doing a dirty action?"

"I shouldn't die that time," said Ossie, and he made a nice ring of smoke in the air.

"You don't know what you are saying."

"I know I'd do anything rather than die; so would anybody; and it's all bosh saying they wouldn't. People nowadays ain't such fools as to die if they can help it. Everybody looks after himself, when it comes to the point. You'd do anything to save your life, just as I would."

"God forbid!" said Dick.

"Well I make no pretence," said Ossie

as loftily as if he were on the highest moral
ground.   "I'd do anything to save my
life; and there isn't a fellow at the Club
who wouldn't say just as I do.   The fact
is,.Dick, you ain't a man of the world."

"Well, I don't desire your death," said
Dick.

"And I don't desire yours," said Ossie;
"and I advise you, if you see any danger,
to run——"

"Like a hare?" suggested Dick.

"I like a nice warm comfortable life,"
continued his cousin; "and it's getting
beastly chilly here; and I'm going back
to bed.   Good-night, Dickie, you old brute.
Everybody for himself! and *Sauve qui
peut!*   That's the thing in these days.
Chacun pour soi! and the Devil take the
hindmost!"

Mr Langdon's knowledge of the French
language was of the slightest, but he spoke
it with a very pretty accent.   On the present

occasion his French precepts sounded so pretty in his ear, that further argument seemed unnecessary. Ossie felt himself one of the wise and good, as, repeating delicately, "*Sauve qui peut! Chacun pour soi!*" he inserted himself carefully into his narrow camp - bed and nestled down for warmth.

Dick, left alone, sat staring out into the night. "If 'twere now to die, 'twere now to be most happy," his lips murmured. Then he sat upright and threw his arms outward and backward with a movement full of life and energy. "What's the matter with me?" he said aloud, and laughed. It seemed strange that he, of all people, should sit so long motionless, mooning, and even muttering poetry. He wondered if he were going to be ill. He never remembered to have been so wakeful before. He began to consider what he should do, if taken ill there and then, he found himself unable to ride forward; and as he began to consider, he caught himself yawning widely. Perhaps he was not so wakeful after all. He would give sleep another chance. So he rose and felt his way through the darkness of the tent; and his head was scarcely on his pillow, before he fell into a deep sleep, and dreamed no more. He never stirred, until the tent was full of mellow light, and Fabian Deane, booted and spurred, stood dark in the doorway with the bright morning behind him, and shouted to the sluggards.

CHAPTER XXIV.

IT needed but a breath to kindle Fabian Deane into one blaze. Dick, who had carefully counted for days past all the people whom he saw, dropped the remark that the land, through which they were riding, could certainly support more inhabitants.

" More !" cried Fabian after gazing sternly on his friend for at least a minute ; " millions !" and with a sudden pressure of the knees he brought his old horse in great astonishment to the side of Dick's animal. He fastened his hot eyes on Mr Hartland's face, eager as he always was for an opportunity of excitement. Fabian was just beginning to find the life a little dull, and to comfort himself with the thought that he could not live without zealous action. For the last few days he had been amusing himself by trying to imitate the Arab seat on horseback. He had succeeded in imitating the Arab head-gear, and glared from under the striped silk like the fiercest of Bedouin warriors.

"Why should not all this land flow again with milk and honey?" he asked with his grand manner, and throwing his arm abroad.

"I wish it would flow with a little more water," said Dick. "If one could secure water, and a fixed limit to taxation, it wouldn't be a bad field for immigration."

"It's a sublime idea," cried Fabian; "the wilderness shall blossom like a rose; it shall be once more fitly called the Holy Land."

"South country labourers might stand the heat well enough," said Dick thoughtfully. "They might learn to shade the backs of their necks; and to sleep at noon;

and—What's the effect of cider in a hot climate?"

"I should like to try," said Ossie. It was the first sign of life which he had given for some time. He was sitting loosely in his saddle, and holding a large white umbrella over his head. His flannel coat was all unbuttoned; his breeches were unbuttoned at the knee; the gaiters, which he had taken off, hung on his horse's neck, and his slippered feet were hanging out of the stirrups. He presented an appearance sufficiently demoralised. It was very hot. They had been riding since early morning low down along the shore of the Sea of Galilee. The high hill on the left seemed to keep the air from them; and the sun now high over their heads blazed in the oleander blossoms, by which they rode. But the greater the heat, the more quickly kindled to enthusiasm was Fabian Deane. He too like the oleander flowers seemed to throb with fierce sunlight.

"It's a great idea," he cried again; "here is a land well nigh empty; there is our little England full to the brim of struggling humanity. What is necessary? An idea! In a moment we infuse the torpid East with Western blood."

"A pretty long moment!" said Dick laughing, though his pulse quickened, as he thought that he really might do something; he felt glad of his friend's belief. "We must wait till we get to Damascus," he added, "and see Tisley. Old Peter says that nobody knows this country like Cavendish Tisley. If he can get me a good title, and a guarantee against over-taxation, I'll buy a bit of land, and send over a bailiff and a few labourers to try the experiment."

"You will?" cried Fabian in amazement.

"Of course," said Dick; "I've been thinking of it for weeks; and it's worth trying."

"Thinking of it! Yes, but—by heaven Dick, I think you are the most wonderful man in the world!" His voice rose as he spoke, till the last words rang in the air.

Dick blushed and looked round uneasily, as if he heard his fame trumpeted to the four quarters of the world. Then he laughed, and said he hoped that it wasn't "as bad as all that."

"You seem to think," said Fabian glaring at him, "that to think of a plan, and to carry it out is all the same thing."

"Well, you must think of it first. That's the hard part. It's easy enough to do the right thing, when you've once seen what it is."

"Easy! It's the most wonderful thing under heaven, and in earth, and in the deep sea to boot. If I had carried out one millionth part of my plans, I should have transformed the face of Europe long ago."

Dick began to laugh; but Fabian regarded him with a countenance stern and full of awe.

"I believe you to be great," he said.

"O come on," said Dick, and he kicked his gallant old steed in the side.

Fabian leaned towards him, and laid his hand on his gaudy bridle. "I must tell you," he said frowning. "It is great of you to be always making plans for the good of others. Your life is attuned to the great harmonics; it's sacred to the sacrifice of self. It's great. That's what it is!"

"Don't talk nonsense," said Dick impatiently. "What do I sacrifice? I like making experiments; I like to make people happy if I can; I've got the means to satisfy my tastes; I'm the luckiest fellow in the world."

"By heaven I think you are!"

"And I hate talking about myself."

"I wish you'd talk about luncheon," said

Ossie plaintively; "how much further, Piero?"

"It is close to," answered the dragoman with his quick responsive grin.

"And yonder," added Fabian with a quick change to his mock-heroic manner,—"lo! yonder I descry our men, and our tents, our mules, and our she-asses."

Piero shook his head. "Those are of the American Principe," he said.

"The American what!" cried Mr Deane; "art thou then unaware, O most ignorant of Maltese dragomans, that there is but one thing which America cannot send us—and that that one thing is a Principe?"

Piero answered only by a smile. He had a great dislike to admitting any gap in his extensive knowledge; he determined to approach again and with cunning diplomacy this question of American princes, and to arrive at the truth without displaying his ignorance. Meanwhile he smiled a smile

of double meaning; and he changed the
subject by becoming suddenly aware of the
well, whereby they were to rest. He struck
spurs to his long-suffering little animal,
and galloped forward.

Beautiful indeed it was in the eyes of the
dusty travellers, this mid-day resting-place,
when at last they reached it. They came
riding out of the dust and the downright
glare of the sun; and there at the foot of a
hill welled up from the cool depths of earth
the fairest of fountains. The clear water
was bound in by rocks; some of which
had been moved from their natural place,
that the precious liquid might escape but
slowly through a mere crevice, and so
run trickling away. All over the rocks,
stooping for moisture, glistening and cool,
crouched an old fig-tree; and the fruit—
perhaps before any other figs in the world
—was already swelling on the boughs.

Dick gave a shout of welcome; he swung

himself out of the saddle, and in a moment
was lying along the largest bough of the
fig - tree. Ossie looked for the most comfortable stone, and so disposed himself that
he could dip his face in the water without
further movement. Fabian settled himself
in the shade with his back against the old
gnarled trunk. After the heat and the
thirst there could be no place more luxuri-
ous in all the world ; and, when Piero had
provided the travellers with their frugal
luncheon, all three felt for a time an almost
perfect contentment. It was a very beautiful place—a place of sweet waters in a
thirsty land—and it was here that Dick
saw, or fancied that he had seen, bright
eyes look at him for a moment with humorous questioning. Ossie had fallen asleep
on the long flat stone with his cheek close
to the water; and Dick looking drowsily
down upon him was more and more occupied by the thought, that without moving

on his branch he could touch his cousin's
head with his left hand. When he had
thought of this sufficiently, he lazily put
out his hand, and held it over the unconscious sleeper's head, smiling with the delightful knowledge that by the slightest
further movement he could plunge Ossie's
head into the crystal basin. While he hung
thus, like doubtful fate in a fig-tree, he was
aware of a noise of hooves. Looking up he
saw four horses and their riders passing at
no great distance. There was a tall man
riding with long stirrups, and a seat rather
military; a young girl mysterious in a
great veil ; another woman, who to the
idlest glance was revealed as a lady's-maid,
and moreover a French one ; and finally
the dragoman. There was an interchange
of rapid chatter between this last and Piero ;
the tall gentleman raised his hand towards
his wide felt hat ; and leaving nothing but
a puff of dust the party had passed away.

Dick had not had time to move; he had only withdrawn the hand, which had been hovering over his cousin's head, and had passed it over his own eyes. Now he lay there drowsy, stretched along the bough, till Fabian Deane, wide awake and instantly restless, began shouting—"To horse!"

CHAPTER XXV.

ONE day, as the three friends were riding onward together, Dick burst out laughing. His was a laugh, which conciliated most people; and which never failed to excite the curiosity of Fabian Deane.

"What is it?" cried Fabian, already on the broad grin with sympathy; "what are you laughing at?"

Dick opened his mouth to answer, but he presently shut it again. He was astonished at his own silence; he was annoyed to find himself blushing under the fixed gaze of his friend, who was now regarding him with solemn inquiry. It was Dick's habit to answer questions without hesitation; and after all, that which had moved his laugh-

ter now was but a small matter. He had
been thinking how childish he must have
looked, hanging in a fig-tree, and debating
whether he should duck his unconscious
cousin or no. Any one, who had chanced
to see him so for the first time, must have
carried away a comical impression of him.
He could not help wondering, if he had
seen a real look of amusement and curiosity; if it were possible to have observed
so much in a moment through a big veil,
which was tied all over the hat and the hair;
if he had really seen eyes, and why he
thought that they must be blue. Considering
such questions, as he rode through a monotonous land, he had begun to laugh; the
friend who watched him like an admiring
and inquisitive collie, had asked him why;
and much to his own amazement he had
not answered. He laughed again, but less
naturally, and shouted to Ossie some frag-
ment of their old school chaff.

One morning Dick and Fabian sat on
their horses, and watched the rapid packing
of tents, furniture, luggage, and kitchen on
the much-enduring mules and asses; while
Ossie, with his bedroom falling around him,
was struggling with a stiff strap of his portmanteau, and warbling pathetically. The
daily scene was always amusing. The mule-
teers were always in a tremendous hurry,
though there was no need for haste; and in
the midst of these childlike persons, who
played the same game every morning and
never were tired of it, the little wrinkled
Coptic cook, superior to the bustle, packed
his bright pans with calm deliberation. As
Dick and Fabian sat watching the well-
known scene, their brown keen-eyed dragoman, who had been galloping hither and
thither and shouting commands, as if there
were really somebody who did not know
exactly what to do, reined in his little steed
beside them, smiling a conciliatory smile.

Smiling his best he pointed away across a little valley, down into which the sunlight still was creeping. They looked where he pointed, and were aware of something white beyond a wrinkle of the low hill westward —something that shone silver white, as the sun's rays caught it.

" That American!" said Piero.

" The encampment of the Principe Americano!" cried Fabian.

Piero smiled, as if he knew a great deal more than he could be induced to make public. He had not yet been able to discover the real truth about the princes of America; and a true instinct warned him, that from Mr Deane at least he would gain nothing but a bombastic fiction.

As Dick sat and looked across the valley to that gleaming speck of white, he felt a hand stroking his knee, and looking down saw a little brown boy who had crept up from the neighbouring mud-village. The

hand left off stroking the cords and was
extended in the usual fashion; the soft
Syrian eyes assumed their most imploring
expression, and the little voice murmured
that one word of Arabic which all travellers
learn so quickly. Dick patted the thin little
shoulder, which the tattered shirt left bare;
and then he dropped a Turkish coin — a
strange little concave circle of pewter with
a hole in it—into the little hand. As the
dark face flushed with joy, it suddenly occurred to Dick that he had done something,
which would commend itself to a young
woman of quick sympathy. It was a strange
thought, but pleasant.

Day after day the three friends jour-
neyed, without adventure, but with much
enjoyment. Once they passed a well,
whereby the day before had been a skir-
mish between Druses and some Maronite
villagers. Once they passed a long string
of Circassians, men, women, and children,

transplanted on a sudden from Europe, that
they might slay and be slain in quarrels
with the Arabs beyond Jordan, and so con-
tribute to the peace of their lord the Sultan.
Such things were events in the travellers'
quiet life. Quiet it was; and yet the
healthy movement onward, far apart from
all the movements of the troubled time, had
a peculiar charm, which they all felt in
some degree. All day they rode on path-
less levels; on barely-marked tracks; on
dry water-courses. In the evening resting
in their tents they would wonder what was
going on in the busy world; how this man
was getting on; if that man were engaged
yet; what was the exact state of things
political. To this last question the excitement, which they had left behind in England, lent peculiar fascination. It was
probable that in the world of journals and of
politicians wonderful rumours were flying
about. Not a letter nor a paper could by

any means reach them—not a rumour.
Any evening, as they sat silent or idly
speculating, a battle might be raging, which
would alter the face of Europe. At that
moment the old empire of the Turks might
be even at an end; and who could foretell
the consequences? Fabian would lash himself to excitement over the extraordinary
contrast between his ignorance of events, and
the events which might already be. What
if the armistice were ended, and the Russians already in Stamboul? What if the
future of this very land, in which he
stretched his legs after a long day's riding, were already settled? He gave his
imagination free play, till Ossie nearly
yawned his head off, and Dick said for
the hundredth time that they were sure to
find news at Damascus. If there were a
British protectorate of Palestine, it would
help his plan of purchasing an estate there.
And then friend Fabian would wax elo-

quent on the awakening from so long sleep;
on the blossoming of the wilderness; the
extinction, by fire if necessary, of the ac-
cursed usurer, and of the pasha's tax-gath-
erer. He always returned to Dick's plan of
land-purchase with a double portion of enthusiasm. He expressed an absolute reverence for his friend. He enjoyed this feeling
of all things. Oxford with all its professors
had afforded him no object of reverence.
London, Europe, the Round World itself
had failed to supply him with a person-
ality sufficiently venerable. But in the
pupil, whom he had intended to form, he
had slowly learned to recognise the Master,
whom he could follow. This was the rare
man—the ideal of the Moral Philosopher—
who, seeing truly and desiring rightly, could
not but form the best purpose, and trans-
late it incontinently into the best action.
Mr Deane hugged himself for joy of this
incomparable treasure. The diver had risen

prince-like with his pearl, and was conscious in every nerve of its value. What pleasure could be compared for a moment with the excitement of watching, even of assisting the experiments of this sanguine youth? What stay was equal to this boy's strong faith? Fabian announced aloud that he warmed both hands at the fire of his friend's life. Indeed he was always getting up little fires, vigorously puffing with the bellows of his enthusiasm, that he might warm those nervous restless hands. "Look at me," he would cry, debasing himself for artistic love of a strong contrast,—"a creature blown about by every wind; with half-a-dozen fragments of faculties; a napkin full of useless talents; a miserable creature who can *do* nothing." Thereupon he would convulsively press his knees upon his astonished quadruped, and leap forward with his chin in the air, his eyes flashing, and the manner of a victorious paladin.

Wonderful are the compensations of life.
As Fabian Deane humbled himself with
pleasure more and more keen before the
feet of Dick Hartland, he himself was becoming an object of interest in the eyes of
his other companion. Ossie felt a need of
talking about himself to somebody; and, as
Dick would only laugh at his sentiment, he
began to turn to Fabian, and to forget that
he hated him. He had acquired a habit of
condemning Mr Deane unheard, for having
come between his cousin and himself. But
habits were mislaid, like gloves, by Ossie;
and Dick was not greatly surprised when
he saw his two companions draw daily
nearer to each other. Dick knew well
enough, when he observed the pathos of
his cousin's looks and the wide stern eyes
of the listener, that a sentimental history
was being poured into a sympathetic ear.
Dick knew that history, so far as it was
constant; he was well aware that what had

been was not always accurately distinguished
from what might have been ; that the whole
tangled skein changed colour, like a pigeon's
breast, with the angle of the sunlight.

"Why have I never known what a
charming fellow your cousin is ?" asked
Fabian sternly one evening. "I have never
met a more delightful nature — so frank !
He told me everything about himself—
everything ; I might have been his brother ;
I wish I were. I have never had so delightful a compliment as his ready confidence—
never in my life !"

"I say," said Ossie on that same night,
as he was undressing himself on the opposite side of the tent, "your friend Deane is
the best fellow I ever met. He is full of
soul. I like fellows with souls. And how
well he talks !"

"You looked as if you were doing all the
talking," said Dick sleepily from his bed.

"Oh, if you are going to be disagreeable,"

said Mr Langdon ; he said no more, until after a few minutes he felt constrained
to add,—"That's just the difference with a
really sympathetic chap."

"Good-night, Ossie," said Dick, and was
presently asleep.

"I wish I had always had such a friend,"
murmured Ossie pathetically ; "I should
have been a better fellow—perhaps." His
sense of pathos would have been heightened, had he known that his cousin, whose
heart should have been melted by his words,
was already far away in the depths of slum-
ber, and was not even dreaming of him.

CHAPTER XXVI.

SINCE dawn they had been riding through
a dreary land. The plain lay behind
them and around them, flat and barren,
deformed by crumbling stones and squalid
scrub. The dust rose powdery from their
horses' feet, and the fierce hot sun beat
downright on their brains. They rode
without speech, and all about them grim
silence brooded in the fiery air. Then
little by little a look of listening came into
their faces; it was hard to be sure if they
heard anything or no. Then little by little
grew upon the ear a sound of many waters.
The jaded beasts quickened their pace un-
bidden. Then, like a mirage to a thirsty

traveller in the desert, was a vision of waving green, a gleam of silver; and presently
the three young men were riding by a river,
which was sparkling here and there below
them, hurrying with glad rush of shadowed
waters through moving shade. There was
shade all the way; for in long line on either
bank slender trees stood close together;
and trees had pushed down knee-deep into
the stream, drinking refreshment and waving their delicate green heads; even the
trees seemed to be hastening forward, down
to the city of fountains.

" Praise be to God," murmured Fabian,
" who laveth the thirsty land."

Then they all began to talk; and presently Ossie fell to humming a little French
air, eloquent of youth and love. And so
a little above the happy rushing river they
rode, with new life and light-hearted, till
Piero, who was cunning showman enough
to present his best effects without previous

warning, pointed suddenly and with dramatic fire up a dusty hill, and said briefly—
" From that top, Damascus ! "   Fabian
caught fire in an instant, dashed his animal at the hill, and was half-way up the
slope before Ossie had grasped the dragoman's meaning.

When they had all reached the top, they
were all silent for a time.   The stream of
trees, by which they had been riding, came
forth beneath them from the mouth of the
valley, and spread like a large fan, luxuri-
ant and freshly green, wide into the dry
barren plain.   Slender minarets rose among
the trees; and everywhere was the shy
gleaming of water.   Tired of glare and
dust they looked down from their barren
height upon an earthly paradise.

After a time Ossie began softly to sing
his little French romance.   Dick got off
his horse and loosened the girths.   Fabian
still sat motionless and silent in his saddle ;

and in his mind rose some tale of the young
Mahomet, gazing down on this city of fair
waters, and thereafter turning away to the
desert and to the choice of a paradise more
spiritual.

" A great sight, sir ! " said a strange voice.

They turned and recognised the American traveller who had passed them by
the fig-tree. A little further to the right
they could see his horses, and the young
lady attended by the maid and dragoman.
The father had come to make friends ; and
he had the air of a man whose offers of
friendliness were always well received. He
stood upright with his wideawake in his
hand, and his smile showed a set of teeth
very white and regular. His fresh colour
and clear blue eyes made him look younger
than he was ; but he was saved from an
excessive youthfulness by the unconcealed
baldness of the top of his head. For the
rest, his hair was soft and brown ; and his

face was shaved so scrupulously, that viewed
in connection with the difficulties of travel
and the lazy influence of the Levant it suggested no little care of his personal appearance. The admirable cut of the spotless
nankeen clothes, which hanging loose seemed
yet to fit so well the tall straight figure,
conveyed the same suggestion.

Indeed there seemed every reason why
his advances should be well received; and
it is certain that he expected a good recep-
tion. The young Englishmen did not dis-
appoint him. Indeed Mr Deane, who was
given to inveigh with quite disproportion-
ate fierceness against the Insular reserve
and cold manners of his countrymen, pro-
voked a look of amused wonder in the tall
stranger's blue eyes by the desperate earn-
estness of his address. He did the hon-
ours of the view, as if he had never been
anywhere else. The torrent of words, which
seemed to trip over each other, of unfinished

sentences and eager interjections, which
were intended to prove the absence of all
British pride and suspicion, were comically
contrasted with the few deliberate utterances of the American.

Ossie listened to the dialogue with lips
softly whistling; while Dick was wondering whether the girl, who never looked that
way, was aware that her father was talking to them. He wondered what she was
thinking about. He fancied that there was
something melancholy in her air, as she
looked away to the city of gardens, and
beyond the city to the boundless breadth
of dusty plain. She was so far away, that
he could not see the expression of her face;
but as he idly watched her, he saw her
raise a handkerchief for a moment to her
eyes. He wondered if the action was
caused by the dust.

"I expect that we shall meet again at
the Hotel," said their new acquaintance.

"O yes "—" of course "—" I hope so," said the three young men ; and they turned their horses as they spoke, and rode away down the hill.

The hotel, where they alighted in the city of Damascus, was not as other hotels. All round the large square court were crisp green pomegranate shrubs, newly lit with little blossoms, like flames, amid the cool shiny leaves. Behind this row of shrubs was the shady space into which rooms opened on every side; and above this space was the wide covered gallery, into which more rooms opened in like manner. A railing ran round the gallery; and on this railing a lazy man, or a poet imbibing the Orient, might lean all day, stare at the liberal fountain, which splashed in the sunny centre of the court below, and listen to its pleasant music.

In one of the rooms on the ground-floor a daily dinner was prepared for guests, if

there were any in the hotel, and for a few
European dwellers in the town; and in this
sparsely-furnished apartment Dick Hartland
and his friends were seated at the long bare
table, when at the sound of a moving gown
they looked up, and saw the American girl
following her father through the doorway,
which was open at that hour to the softened
evening light. There were no ladies in the
room; but the young girl came in, as one
who is accustomed to the eyes of men. She
seemed unaware of their looks; she was
very neat, cool, and self-possessed. Dick
was disappointed. She was not so pretty
as he had expected. She was pretty, but
by no means beautiful. Yet she was
pretty. The brown hair looked very soft
about her fair low forehead; and the
eyes, which were after all not blue but
grey, had a pleasant expression of interest
and candour. Her eyebrows were arched
and delicate; and her skin was like the

inner side of the rose-leaves. Even Dick,
who had given little thought to the ways
of women, knew in a moment why the big
veil had been worn on the journey. She
was pretty—but after all no prettier than
many other people; and Dick recognised
this fact with a feeling, which was comically like relief. As she seated herself at
the table, he suddenly thought that he was
looking at her too long; but before he
could withdraw his eyes, her eyes had met
them. She gave a little grave bow, as to
her father's friends, and turned to speak to
her father.

"What a delightful little turned-up nose!"
whispered Ossie to Dick.

"Hush!" said Dick shortly; "she'll hear
you."

"What's the odds?" muttered Ossie unabashed; "she'd like it."

After dinner Dick went up-stairs to write
a letter to his mother. After the fulfilment

of this duty as he was crossing the great
court below, he saw the lamplight streaming
through the polished leaves of a pomegranate from an open door behind it. From
the same doorway came the sound of voices;
and as he recognised among them the im-
passioned tones of Fabian Deane, Dick
turned aside and looked into the room.
Two swinging lamps, which were not too
bright, hung from the ceiling, and beneath
them a little fountain splashed in its shal-
low basin. Dick saw at a glance that his
friends were already on the best terms with
their new acquaintance. On one side of
the room the young lady and Ossie were
chatting pleasantly together; while on the
low divan, which ran along the opposite
wall, Fabian was sitting sideways, eager for
information, plying his new friend with
weighty questions about American affairs.
He was amazed by the answers which he
received. Scorn of insular prejudice was

his dominant feeling on that day; he had
been ready to sing second to the most
extravagant praises of the great Western
world, and to accept with a sigh the inevitable comparison with the dear mother
country—the little England who—alas!—
was growing old. But how could he sing
second, if the other would not take the
leading part in the pæan? He found himself prompting the American to laudations
of his country; and the necessity for this
prompting seemed to upset all his established views of the Transatlantic character.
Fabian grew excited, and as his excitement
increased, the other was more critical, more
humorous, more deliberate. Dick came in
with a smile and seated himself to listen.

"It's astounding!" said Fabian to him;
"he doesn't believe in Liberty, or Equality,
or the constitution of the United States, or
—or anything."

The American laughed and laid his hand

on Dick's arm. "You must not think too hardly of me," he said. "Your friend is forcing me to the most heterodox admissions. I fear that I have scared him badly by my doubt, if any two babies were ever born equal." Then as he was rather pleased with the sensation which he had made, and liked a small but intelligent audience, he proceeded to assure them that there was not an educated and sensible American "outside politics," who would not limit the franchise, if he could. Then gliding into a more humorous channel he began to tell them stories about the last political campaign; of the strategy of the Bosses, each in his State; of the ingenious tactics of the city "wire-pullers;" of the tapping of "the barrel" in doubtful districts; of the Irish vote and the consumption of whisky; of paid agents, and sub-agents, and deputy-sub-agents—all voters; of "buldozers" and "repeaters," and other persons prominent

in politics. Afterwards he spoke with un-
abated cheerfulness of the taxes, which he
had to pay; and of the amount of money
which the erection of a single public build-
ing could be made to cost under the foster-
ing care of a city government.

"What a pernicious, incredible, wholly
ghastly state of things!" cried Fabian at last.

"Well," said the American, "I suspect
that we are rather proud of it. It's on a
big scale. It causes us to realise the greatness of our country. We really do think
that there is no other country, which could
afford to be so badly governed."

"You are the most extraordinary American," said Mr Deane, as if he were person-
ally offended.

"I don't think I should have known you
were an American," said Dick.

"I presume that you mean that for a
compliment," said their new acquaintance
with another smile.

"No," said Dick, "I said it because I think it."

"Ah! That's better," said the other.

"If you knew Dick," said Ossie plaintively from the other side of the room, "you'd know that compliments ain't much in his line."

Dick looked across at Ossie, and saw that the grey eyes of the girl, with whom his cousin had been talking so busily, were regarding him with a frank questioning look. As she did not turn her eyes away, he rose and walked across the room to her.

"I have been telling your friend," she said, "that he ought to go to Newport. He's just the kind of Englishman to have a good time at Newport. He would be such a belle."

"I shan't go till you are back in America," said Ossie with a nod.

"When do you think of going back?" asked Dick.

"I wish you could get her to answer that," said her father. "You don't know the lamentable condition of man on our side of the water. We were under the fond delusion that we had abolished slavery; but until the American woman is abolished, there will be no freedom for American men. I am now being dragged around the world—luckily it is not a very large one, as worlds go — because this young lady is tired of Boston; and New York; and Newport; and tired of dancing the German; of summer picnics; of winter sleigh-rides; of——"

The girl looked up quickly with the pretty eyebrows raised and the underlip a little pouting. "Well?" he asked.

As they looked at each other, father and daughter both began to smile. Then she put her arm through his, as if she would lead him away.

"Hold on a minute!" he said; "I wish

to present myself to these gentlemen. My name is Holcroft—Henry Holcroft of Boston; and this is my daughter Kitty,—whom I ought to have named first, as she is by far the more important person."

Then they all laughed, and Dick made haste to introduce himself and his friends, not without embarrassment. Mr Holcroft bowed to each as his name was mentioned; assured them collectively of his pleasure at having met them, and so departed with his daughter.

"That's a clever girl, if you like," said Ossie.

The suggestion of cleverness came with a slight shock to Dick. He was just thinking what an arch innocent face it was.

CHAPTER XXVII.

DAY followed day; and neither the Holcrofts nor the three young Englishmen seemed in a hurry to leave Damascus. There were reasons enough for delay. The American showed a fine taste for inlaid armour and embroidered silks, and spent hours at a time in the narrow ways of the Bazar. In that all-day twilight he found the atmosphere of antiquity, which, as he liked to declare, gave him a livelier pleasure, than anything else which he had experienced in his travels. He would stand looking down one of these long shaded alleys, in which perhaps a single shaft of light fell through the boards above straight upon

a booth of brilliant colours; and standing
there he would remind his young friends
again and again that they might have found
the same scene—the same in all its details
—on any day in any year of any century,
when they had "happened to come along."
He would admit no limitation to the absolute changelessness, with which he pleased
his fancy. He seemed almost serious in
his assertion that the turbaned slumbrous
sellers, who sat cross-legged on their booths,
had sat there when the good Haroun Al-
raschid was Caliph in Bagdad. With these
same solemn merchants he was never tired
of making bargains. He rejoiced to see
them roused to sudden life, like old snakes
on the introduction of a rabbit, by the first
suggestion of barter. He would furnish his
dragoman with new and fantastic objections
to the thing which he intended to buy, and
would listen with childlike pleasure to the
protestations translated to him. After all

his bargaining his only fear seemed to be that his attendant, who entered keenly into the sport, would insist on the harmless old gentlemen parting with their goods too cheap. Indeed he was so generous with his money, that it was not long before the court of the hotel became itself a centre of commerce, where grave merchants were found motionless and smoking at all hours of the day.

If Mr Holcroft lingered in Damascus for love of the antique, his new friends had even stronger reasons for delay. It was pleasant to stay in one place after daily journeying, and to talk to new people after so long an experience of each others' conversation; but these reasons were only good enough for Ossie. Weightier matters detained his comrades. They had made the acquaintance of Mr Cavendish Tisley; and though Mr Tisley had said but little, he had listened with interest to

Dick's plan of purchasing an estate in Palestine. Cavendish Tisley was a great listener. As he sat attentive, with his capacious forehead bowed a little forward, it was almost impossible not to credit him with great powers of thought. He was not tall, but he was very solemn and deliberate; and if he was a little stout, so was the great Napoleon. He was almost always booted; he was given to riding through the adjacent country, sitting solid in the saddle, and staring. His steadfast gaze was almost as impressive, as his air of attentive listening. Why Cavendish Tisley lived in Damascus no man knew,—and no woman; for Mrs Tisley was content with wonder; and this wonder was part of that vast admiration, with which she regarded her silent lord. The less he told her, the more she admired him. She gave him credit for thoughts so profound, that they would shatter her poor intellect; for

schemes so far-reaching, that her imagination could not comprehend them. She
knew that he was a student, or rather a
master of the Eastern Question. To his
mental powers and to his rides, which she
gratefully acknowledged to be also good for
his health, she ascribed his exhaustive knowledge of the hardest problem of modern
politics. She asked to know no more. She
watched him ride forth, and come in; and
she had his slippers ready, when he divested
himself of those stupendous boots. A few
facts connected with the sojourn of Mr
Tisley in Damascus were indeed known to
a few select persons. It was known that
he wrote occasional letters to a friend in
London. It was known moreover that this
friend was a Member of Parliament. Now
this Member never lost an opportunity of
speaking in any debate connected, however
slightly, with The Eastern Question; and
he had acquired no slight reputation for

his knowledge of "public opinion on the
spot." Public opinion on the spot, whether
the spot in question were in Bagdad, Jerusalem, Stamboul, or even in the mountains
of Thessaly, was represented in the mind of
that eloquent legislator by Mr Cavendish
Tisley. Mr Tisley had once talked with an
Arab chief from beyond Jordan ; and more
than once he had paid a visit, patronising
and mysterious, to a venerable but servile
sage and conjurer, who lived near him in
Damascus. To such a man Dick's plan of
buying a few acres was of course a small
matter. He smiled not unkindly, but a
little sadly, as if he too would like to be
able to interest himself in these trifles of
every day. After twenty - four hours he
committed himself to the statement, that
it was impossible to say whether the little
plan could be carried out or not. When
two more days had gone, he promised to
make inquiries; and he hinted with due

solemnity that he must await some secret information from Constantinople. Meanwhile at Constantinople itself nothing exciting had occurred. On the downs about the city the Russian and Turkish armies confronted each other, as they had been confronting each other for many weeks. There was no collision ; and the armistice was maintained. Fabian Deane would occasionally cry out in amazement that after all their journeying where no news could reach them, after all their mighty speculations about great events in progress, they had come out from the world of wonder to find that nothing whatever had happened since they left the world of facts.

Dick Hartland was quite content to wait for further information about the possibility of his purchase. Ossie wondered that his cousin, who was so uncomfortably energetic, could stay quiet in a place where there was so little to do ; and when he expressed his

wonder, Dick was a little surprised himself
that he found Damascus so interesting.
There was little to see except flowers and
fountains; green trees amid the low white
houses; minarets like slender cypresses for
life and beauty; fine oval faces of young
boys and girls with faint rose-bloom on
clear dark skins, delicate straight features
and long lovely eyes; and the loose bright-
coloured raiment of wrinkled elders. A
string of camels entering a narrow lane of
the Bazar with dignified looks and paces,
treading the dust mottled by specks of sunlight with their widespread silent feet, was
the chief event of a day. Certainly there
was little to do in Damascus, and no objects
to visit; and yet Dick found the place
interesting. Perhaps his contentment was
in great part due to the society of Mr Holcroft. He felt a strong sympathy with his
new friend's good temper and pleasant
humour; and he liked to gain information

about American people and American land
from a man, who knew a good deal and
told it so pleasantly. Mr Holcroft was
emphatically interesting. Then there was
his daughter too. She seemed like her
father, and yet unlike. She was not
always so frankly pleasant. Dick thought
that he could read the father at a glance;
but the daughter puzzled him a little.
She did not say much to him; and when
he was talking with her father, though
she sometimes listened with a face bright
with interest, she more often stood quiet
with an absent look in her grey eyes, and
perhaps a slight smile on the mouth, which
seemed to the young man like a rose-bud.
Once or twice, when he was speaking, his
eyes met hers, and his words were checked
for a moment by her look. It struck him
that she was not attending to his arguments; but that she was rather regarding
him with a calm interest, as if she wondered

what sort of man he was. He did not object; he had nothing to hide; he hoped she thought well of him. He did not know what he thought of her, except that she was spoiled by her father. However she too was interesting.

CHAPTER XXVIII.

ONE morning Dick came out of his room
with a long day's idleness before him, and
not in the least annoyed by the prospect.
He was full of life ; and yet he was content
to do nothing, but loaf about and look at
the strange people and bright colours, the old
doorways in shadow, and the camel in the
street. Certainly none of his relations and
friends would have predicted this leisurely
temper in Dick Hartland.

Dick went and leaned on the railing and
looked down into the court, which usually
furnished something or somebody to look
at. Now however it seemed to be empty ;
and the young man was idly noting how

sharp was the edge of the shadow, which at
that early hour left but a narrow strip of
whiteness on the pavement, when he was
aware of another spectator. He could see
Miss Holcroft sitting under the balcony on
his left. One of the pomegranate tubs had
been moved for her convenience ; and it had
left for her sketching a bit of the court, the
fountain, and beyond the fountain the shrubs
and the overhanging gallery. Dick watched
her a little while, silent in air above her,
and smiling, childishly enough, with pleasure
because she did not know that anybody was
looking at her. He knew that girls were
supposed to put on airs and graces, when
they knew that men were looking at them.
So he smiled to himself — and he smiled
too, because she seemed to complete the
picture before him so prettily.

After a time he began humming an old
English air ; and he was still humming
with a delightful consciousness of wellbeing,

when he strolled down the stairs and crossed the court towards the young artist. Miss Holcroft did not seem to put on any airs and graces in honour of the young Englishman. She paused for a moment, with her brush in the air, to give him a little nod of welcome; then she turned her eyes again to the scene before her, and even screwed them up a little in her effort to see it exactly as it was. It was clear that she was in a very conscientious mood.

"You seem to be always at work," said Dick, standing leisurely behind her with his hands dropped idle in his coat-pockets.

"I am tired of doing nothing," she said; "I've been doing nothing all my life."

"Not a very long time!" murmured Dick; and, as she took no notice of this comment, he added presently, "You went in tremendously for society in America, I suppose?"

She pouted, and looked critically at

her sketch with her head on one side. "Society went in for me," she said, as she put a touch very carefully on the paper.

Dick laughed : " And you didn't dislike it, I suppose ? " he asked.

"Dislike it ! I had a splendid time—for two seasons. But two seasons are enough for any girl. At the end of the second season I knew just what everybody would say. They said very sweet things; but I was tired of sweets. I told papa that, if I stayed for a third season, I should go mad." She spoke rather slowly, and she paused after every sentence while she attended to her painting. Dick had supposed that all American women had high disagreeable voices, but the voice of this girl at least seemed sweet and rather low. She laid great emphasis on the word " very," and the accent on the first syllable of " papa ; " but trifles such as these seemed delicate touches, which for the young Englishman only heightened her individuality, her distinction. Dick never for a moment supposed that there were many American girls like this one. There might be many prettier, or cleverer, or more independent; but this girl was peculiar. He was sure that, wherever she might be, she was not like other girls. Certainly she was interesting.

"And don't you ever sigh for the balls and parties and things?" asked Dick presently.

"Never," she answered. "Cousin Hatty has written me all winter whole volumes full of dances—and bouquets—and beaux —and who's attentive to who—and it's *very* interesting; but I never wish I was there. I bequeathed Hatty all my partners, and flowers. When I go home, I shall be *passée;* I shall do art needlework."

"When do you think you shall go back?"

"We shan't go home for at least a year."

"But don't you hate missing Newport? Isn't that the place where they have everything—even hunting in summer? Isn't it an awfully jolly place?"

"Newport is heavenly."

"Very well then?"

"I told you that I was tired of amusing myself." She seemed to be tired of sketching for the time being; for she laid her block on one side. Then she looked up at Dick with that little pout of the underlip, which he was beginning to recognise, and said— "Ah, Mr Hartland, I see that you think me frivolous." At the moment Dick was thinking her charming. She seemed so frank and natural, that they were like old friends.

"Not too frivolous," he said.

"I suppose I am frivolous," she observed with an air of gravity. "I like to feel that I am dressed perfectly. I like attentions.

That's why I could never be happy in England."

" Why not ?   I am sure you could."

" No.   In England the men expect the attentions.   Wouldn't you be shocked, as an Englishman, if I sent you for some clean water for my painting ? "

" I should run," said Dick ; " but haven't you painted enough ?   You are always absorbed in something ? "

" I came abroad to improve myself," she said.   " You are not running very fast ; and you needn't ; I won't paint any more. One way of improving oneself is to talk to intelligent foreigners."

" Thank you for the compliment," said Dick.

" Oh you don't know what an interesting specimen you are.   Mr Langdon told me that you are a squire.   I never quite realised that there were squires outside of your English novels."   She regarded Dick, who had seated himself on the edge of the nearest pomegranate - tub, with her frank straightforward look. He laughed, as he assured her that he was not quite sure what a squire was. At this she expressed great surprise.

" You are a landowner, anyhow ? " she asked.

" Yes," answered Dick.

" And you ride around your farms ? "

" I sometimes trot over to see a farmer ? "

" And you—how do you say it ?—you appoint your minister ? "

" My what ? "

" Your—pastor—parson——"

" Clergyman," said Dick. " Yes, there is a living in my gift; but it's disposed of long ago. My mother found the parson. My mother's rather fond of parsons. But you must come yourself and see the place when you come to England. You ought to see an English country-place, you know ;

and I'm sure you'd like Claring. Everybody likes Claring."

"Claring," she repeated: "Claring! What a pretty name! Why, it's perfectly lovely!" She sat musing for a minute. " I wonder if I shall ever go to England. I don't know any English ladies. I should love to know your mother."

There was something in these last words of Miss Holcroft, which startled Dick. There were certain grave thoughts, which always returned to him at the mention of his mother. And now he began to wonder what his mother would think of this girl. So far as he knew, Mrs Hartland had never spoken to an American; but now he suddenly remembered the very time and place, when and where he had heard her speak with grave disapproval of American women, as terribly extravagant, and caring for nothing but dress, and for the attentions of men. He seemed to see his mother, as he had seen her then, standing in all her severe simplicity, mildly regretful for the frivolity of the ladies beyond the sea.

"Well?" said the girl, who had so lately confessed a liking for dress and for attention; and Dick began to laugh.

"You can't go back to the States," he said, "without going through England."

"We can go home from Havre," said she; "and please don't say 'The States.' If there is a thing I cannot endure, it is to hear your countrymen talk about 'the States.'"

"What am I to say?"

"Say 'America.'"

"But there are other places in America besides your —— What shall I call them?"

"There's nothing else that amounts to anything," she said, with her pretty little mutinous air, as she rose and picked up her sketch-book and paint-box.

"Mayn't I carry them for you?" asked Dick.

"Ah," she said, with her eyebrows raised, "you wish to show me that Englishmen can be polite; but I wish to show you that American girls are not all helpless." She gave him a smile and nod for farewell, and moved away,—a light, graceful figure under the shadow of the old gallery.

On the evening of the same day, Dick came in from an aimless ramble through the nearest streets; and as he entered the hotel, it occurred to him that he would look for Miss Holcroft. There were several questions which he would like to ask her. He was curious about social life in America, and her answers were sure to be amusing. Indeed he was already smiling, though he did not know it, while he pictured the changes of her face as she listened to his questions. He found Mr Holcroft and Fabian Deane smoking with oriental calm

the tobacco of Latakia, with their coffee-
cups fragile as egg-shells on the little round
table between them; both were silent, and listening to the drowsy music of the fountain.
Dick made no effort to rouse these energetic
gentlemen from their unwonted lethargy,
but crossed the court to the open door of
the sitting - room. There she was in the
corner, which she had made her own; and
there was Ossie by her side. They were so
much interested, that neither noticed the
new comer in the doorway. Dick turned
away with an unusual feeling of irritation.
For the first time it struck him as un-
manly in Ossie to trade on his appearance
of boyhood and innocence. He had observed long ago that many women treated
his cousin as a boy, and admitted him
easily to a peculiar intimacy on the ground
of his harmlessness. Formerly he had
laughed at this fact; but now it struck
him as a little objectionable. He had a

vision of the little boudoir back-stairs Abbé
with lace ruffles.   He thought that women
ought not to be deceived by this false air
of guilelessness; certainly clever women
ought not to be so deceived for a moment;
if a clever woman did not see through
Ossie, the only possible reason was that
she chose to be blind.   Dick had no doubt
that Miss Holcroft was very clever.   She
must have seen through the imposture of
many men.   Probably she had had a love
affair, or two.   What more likely than that
she was abroad on account of something
of the sort?   How easily the bloom is
brushed away from a girl in the bustle
and crowding of a meanly - ambitious
society!   How quickly she loses that
fine maidenly intuition, which warns her
of the approach of anything not wholly
respectful and refined!   This finest of
feminine powers becomes dull.   She grows
accustomed to coarser flavours, to amuse-

ments ever more and more exciting. To Dick the inevitable effect of worldly society on a young woman seemed at that moment startlingly clear. No nature however naturally fine could withstand the fatal influence. He felt sure that two years ago Miss Holcroft would have shrunk from sitting in a corner with a frivolous young man; that she would have been distressed by his sham sentiment, and his sham simplicity.

Dick's thoughts had been following each other with extraordinary rapidity; and he suddenly awoke to the fact that they were going very far. He found that he was painting the light-hearted cousin, of whom he had always been so fond, in very black colours — and for no reason; for it could hardly be called a reason that he had found him talking pleasantly with a young lady in the cool of the evening. Dick thought that something must be the

matter with himself; but he did not waste
time in considering his own symptoms. He
turned back again, and walked with a careless air into the room. Ossie stopped his
chatter for a moment, nodded, and turned
again to his companion. If the girl's grey
eyes were raised to him, Dick did not
notice them. It struck him that he was
not wanted. He turned over some photographs on the table; he laughed rather
loudly at one of them, which did not
amuse him in the least degree; and then
he sauntered out of the room. Just beyond the threshold he began to whistle
an Italian air inspired by the proverbial
variability of the sex, but he stopped almost
instantly. For a few moments he lingered
in the court, where he could hear the lively
talk of the two young people but not distinguish the words. Why should he care
for the words? Of course they were chat-
tering about dancing and gowns, about

Newport and Paris. He looked back at
the open door, through which the light
streamed softly; then he strode across the
open space, with never a glance for the
numberless bright stars set so far away,
and came to Mr Holcroft and Fabian.
Fabian was aroused from his unusual
silence by the sight of his friend. "To
think that we are in Damascus!" he ex-
claimed.

"Considering the time we have been
wasting here," said Dick, "I wonder you
haven't found it out before." He meant
to speak humorously, but the tone of his
voice was cross; and this was so unusual
a matter, that Fabian raised himself in his
seat and stared at his friend with pene-
trating eyes.

CHAPTER XXIX.

WHEN Dick awoke the next morning, his temper was cheerful as usual. He vaguely remembered that he had been cross on the previous evening—and for no reason. He was in a most interesting place, and with pleasant people; and he meant to enjoy these good things. He could not think what had been the matter with him; he did not care to think. As the cool light of early morning filled his bare room, his spirits rose higher and higher. Perhaps one cause of his elation was that on that day at least there was something definite to be done. Mr Cavendish Tisley had determined to visit a native village, which was at some distance from the city. Nobody knew why Mr Tisley wished to gaze on this particular village. It was enough that his purpose had been formed; and this purpose was chiefly interesting to some of his new acquaintance, because he had offered to be their guide, if they would ride with him. He had appointed an early hour for the start; for it was important to reach the village before the sun was very hot, and to allow plenty of time for the noontide halt, and luncheon in the shade. They were to carry their food on an extra beast. Altogether it was emphatically an expedition; and Dick after leisurely days was excited by the prospect of something to do.

When they were all assembled outside the city, they were so imposing a party, that Mr Tisley would have been almost justified in feeling like a colonel of irregular horse on active service. He sat silent and round on his weedy animal, courteous but grave, and solemnly inspected his troop. The horses of the three young Englishmen seemed unusually lively after their late repose, and shared the gaiety of their riders. Fabian dashed through the dust with the air of an Arab at play. Mr Holcroft ambled up with his long stirrups, and beside him cantered his daughter with her blue veil drawn again about her face. Then Piero and the other dragoman began to exclaim vehemently; Mr Tisley's trusty attendant started the led horse with the provisions; the great Cavendish himself moved slowly forward; the expedition had started.

The sight of the blue veil reminded Dick of the day when he first saw it, of those pleasant moments when he looked from the leaves of a fig-tree and saw a girl ride by. He smiled as he thought, how important a Western girl became in a land, where women seemed beings of another species. After all there was nothing remarkable about this slight American maiden. Dick thought that in London she would be merely one of many pretty girls. He was certain that nobody would even notice her, if Mrs Torington were present; and he tried to recall his cousin Betty's face, and to see it side by side with that of the girl before him. It is probable that he was staring; for presently Miss Holcroft turned towards him with an expression of inquiry. Though her look was grave and contemplative, Dick could not help thinking that she regarded him with some amusement. Several times he had seen her look at him like that—as if, he said to himself, she were observing some rather comical specimen. He thought it a little bold; he could not reconcile it with his idea of a young girl—an idea which included a modest dropping of the eyes, when they met those of a young man—but never-

theless it excited his curiosity. Now he
thought that he would ask her what she
found in him to laugh at; but even, as he
moved in his saddle, Ossie rode up to her
on the farther side, and was greeted with
much animation. As she reined back her
horse, Dick pushed forward and joined her
father. Riding by the side· of Mr Holcroft
he could not only talk with that pleasant
gentleman; but he could also catch occasional fragments of the conversation, which
was carried on in front and rear. In front
he saw Fabian Deane grow more and more
excited, as he rode close beside Mr Cavendish Tisley and spurred him to brief oracu-
lar utterances.

"Only a handful of marines?" cried
Fabian in great surprise; "is that all you'd
want?" and Dick saw Mr Tisley's nod
momentous with the fate of nations.

"They can do everything but dress,"
said Miss Holcroft in the rear—"ah, but

that is very tactless of me; and I do admire them ever so much."

"English girls ain't bad," said Ossie, and Dick wondered if he gave a passing thought to Susan Bond.

"The Druses! Yes, yes?" asked Fabian eagerly.

"They are so strong," said Miss Holcroft, "and have such splendid colour; and they can walk all day; and they ride so well; and they manage the village schools."

"You haven't known many of 'em, have you?" asked Ossie.

"No," she said; "but I know all about them from your English novels."

"Oh," said Ossie, and he began thinking of the society young ladies of his acquaintance, and lazily wondering, how many of them had bright colour, and could walk or ride all day without fatigue.

"It would be a revolution!" cried Fabian, as if a revolution were the most desirable of luxuries; and Cavendish Tisley inclined his head slowly.

As the sun grew hotter, the party became more silent. Even Fabian relapsed into longer periods of burning thought, and contented himself more and more with gazing at his mysterious companion, in whom he was beginning to see one, who should mould the destinies of Asia. They had left the flowering cactus-shrubs behind, and the land, through which they rode, became ever more dry and desolate. At last Mr Cavendish Tisley drew rein, and pointed silently to a low dusty hill before them. Without a guide they might have passed the place, not knowing that it was a village. The low mud hovels, of the same colour as the earth, scarcely broke the outline of the hill. From these human burrows a few lean ragged people crept out to look at them with friendly, though apathetic, faces. Almost all were women and nearly

naked children; for the men were scratching
the ground somewhere, that the fruits of
their labour might be shared between the
Pasha and the City Usurers. Of these
usurers Dick had heard something, which
filled him with righteous indignation; and
now, as he looked at these patient half-
starved faces, he was obliged to relieve his
feelings by abusing these money-lenders to
Mr Holcroft.

"They get some scoundrel of a Vice-
consul to naturalise them," he said; "and
then they use the bullying power of their
adopted Consulate to extort their 20 per
cent; and that's what the Great Powers
do for the benefit of these poor barbarous
Orientals."

"You don't mean so?" said the American, who indeed could scarcely believe this
discreditable fact. Mr Tisley had turned
his head to hear; he neither contradicted
nor confirmed the statement of this young

man, but his heavy face assumed the expression of one who could tell far stranger tales if he chose. He turned his head back again, and sat staring at the village, at which he had come forth to stare. For all his indignation Dick almost laughed aloud, as he looked at the stout gentleman sitting solid on his weedy Arabian, and marked the weight of thought on his brow. It struck him, as it had struck him once or twice before, that Cavendish Tisley's observations of the country were a little interfered with by intrusive thoughts of his legs and their appearance in those portentous boots. From Mr Tisley Dick's eyes wandered to the place where Miss Holcroft sat, withdrawn a little from the party. While he was speaking of the usurers to her father, he had all the time been conscious that she too was listening. He was a little annoyed by the fact that, when she was present, he could not

help thinking of her. Though she were
silent, and even when he would not look
at her, she seemed to make her presence
felt in a perplexing manner. She made
him think of her; and she made him think
of himself—and this was annoying to him,
because it was one of his theories that in
a world, which furnished so much food for
thought, it was a waste of precious time
to think about oneself. However, since the
girl would by no means be ignored, he
allowed his eyes to wander in her direction. She turned her head at once and
looked at him; and he saw with surprise
the bright tears on her eyelashes. She was
sorry for these poor people; and he felt a
quick sympathy with her sorrow. The
next moment he was annoyed again; for
she continued to regard him with a pretty
mutinous look, as if she were asking him
what he thought of her tears, and telling
him at the same moment that she cared

not a jot what he thought. Dick said to himself impatiently that this girl studied effects. Nobody else had seen her tears, for he was between her and the rest of the party; he thought that her position had been deliberately chosen. A minute later she was talking gaily to Ossie, as they all rode briskly forward to the halting-place. Not far away there was a little cluster of palms by the fountain ; and in the shadow of these stately trees Mr Tisley's dusky attendant assisted by the dragomans had prepared the light repast.

They were all rather silent as they rode homeward, thinking many thoughts. One thought recurred again and again to Dick Hartland — it was high time to leave Damascus. He wondered how he could have lingered there so long, when he might have hurried onward to Constantinople, and seen the Russian troops at San Stephano. It was likely enough that he would never

have another chance of visiting Stamboul
at a moment so exciting. As for his plan
of buying a parcel of Syrian land, he felt
more and more doubtful whether he would
gain either information or assistance from
the great Cavendish. He thought that he
had been strangely stupid, because he had
not perceived long ago that he could learn
more in Pera about the future of Palestine,
and the possibility of his model farm.
When they drew near to the city and the
shadows were lengthening, he had made up
his mind to delay no more. He would
speak to his companions that evening; he
did not suppose that they would raise any
serious objections; he felt sure that neither
of them was doing any good there; besides
both had acquired the habit of acquiescing
in his arrangements.

CHAPTER XXX.

THE excellent reasons for leaving Damascus, with which Dick Hartland favoured his friends, did not produce that prompt agreement which he had expected. Fabian and Ossie had come to his room, as he asked them to do ; but when he told them of his wish to depart on the next day, neither seemed in a hurry to express approval of the plan. On the contrary Ossie sat down in silence on Dick's portmanteau and looked sulky ; and Fabian, after contemplating his former pupil for a minute with stern eyes, began to walk up and down the room with his hands behind his back and his lips pressed tight together.

"Well," said Dick to Ossie with an encouraging manner, "don't look as if you'd lost all your friends."

Ossie muttered something, from which his cousin gathered that he doubted if he had any friends, and rather thought that he was not allowed to make any.

"I can't understand you," cried Fabian suddenly, stopping short in his walk and glaring at Dick; "I thought you were so keen about this plan of yours."

"I want to do the thing, if it can be done," said Dick.

"And yet you want to leave this place, where according to universal consent is the one man who knows what can be done in Palestine and Syria—the one man who can help you to do the thing, when he has once pronounced that the thing can be done."

"When!" echoed Dick with a smile which seemed to the other too frivolous

for the subject. Fabian was irritated.
"And what do you want to go for?" he
continued, stopping again in his walk and
wheeling round upon his friend. "Because
some great show may come off at Constantinople, and you not be there to see? Do
you want to gape, like a tourist, at a battle
or an occupation? If there is a battle, what
can you *do?* What can you do, if the Russians march into Constantinople? Gape
like a venerable Cookite at a Raree show?
I can't understand you, who are so practical, so eager to *do* something, and who
actually have a plan for doing something
which ought to keep you here—on the spot
—which—no, it beats me, I confess." And
here Mr Deane shrugged his shoulders,
strode to the window, and stared into the
darkness.

Then Mr Langdon from his place on
the portmanteau lifted up his voice in
turn. "It does seem absurd," he com-

plained, "to go just when one has found at last some decent people to talk to."

Dick looked from one friend to the other. He hardly believed yet that the opposition was serious. As he regarded his cousin's pathetic expression, he was the more determined to bear him away. It occurred to him that it might not be so easy to break off Ossie's idle flirtation at a later stage of growth. He must cut it down at once. When everything was ready, he was sure that Ossie would go with him, probably protesting, possibly sulky, but certain to go. So he turned to Fabian, or rather to Fabian's back, for his face was still persistently turned to the darkness of the street. "I think," said Dick, "that I am much more likely to find out at the Embassy at Therapia about the probable state of Palestine. The more I think of it, the less likely it seems that the country will be sufficiently quiet for starting a farming experiment;

but anyway Therapia's the place to make inquiries."

"Oh, if you prefer official information," said Mr Deane with an accent of superb scorn on the word "official," "to the advice and assistance of a man who knows Palestine—who knows it like his own back-yard—of course there's no more to be said."

"To tell you the truth," said Dick, "I'm getting very sceptical about the great Cavendish. Mr Holcroft says he's a booted fraud."

Mr Deane looked at his friend as if he had spoken blasphemy. "Of course," he said solemnly, "if you quote a man who's utterly cynical——"

"Cynical! He's the most genial man I ever met, and I thought you were devoted to him."

"I don't pretend not to like him; but he has no faith. Hear how he talks about the great principles of his own country—how — he doesn't do anything, and he

doesn't believe in anybody else doing anything; and when he meets a man of force——
—— Holcroft!"

The contrast between Mr Holcroft and
Mr Tisley seemed to be too great for more
complete expression.

"The man of action hasn't done anything
that I know of," said Dick.

There was more sorrow than anger in
the gaze which Fabian fixed upon his
friend. "I am sorry for this," he said;
"I've not been blind to it; I've seen it
growing—this unworthy distrust—this—if
I could only tell you some part of what
he has told me—of plans which include
the co-operation of the great Arab tribes,
of the Druses, of English marines — but
unfortunately my lips are sealed. He is
full of great thoughts; and if you would
only come into the thing heartily, there's
nobody could help him like you. I know
you, Dick; and with this man you might

—you might — good heavens! there's no knowing what you might *not* do!"

"There's one thing I'm going to do," said Dick, "and that is to leave this place to-morrow."

"Then there's no more to be said." After this solemn declaration of the uselessness of speech, and a brief pause distinguished by a silence even more full of solemnity, Mr Deane broke forth and spoke for half an hour, almost without cessation, vehemently, eloquently. As he spoke, he became much excited by the pictures which he drew. He walked up and down, glaring, occasionally even gesticulating, as he fancied Syria and Palestine redeemed by the joint action of Cavendish Tisley and Richard Hartland, and the whole land one garden for fertility on the model of the latter's model farm. Dick's little scheme was by no means to be dropped; but it was to be part of some great plan, of which the account was suffi-

ciently fragmentary and mysterious. But
Fabian believed in this great plan for the
regeneration of the East; it was all complete in one colossal mind; there was only
one Tisley, and Fabian on that evening was
his prophet. What glowing visions he
beheld! To what great hopes did he abandon himself in a frenzy of self-abandon-
ment! At last when he had worked himself up to the greatest possible heat, he
began to cool by degrees; and under the
influence of the reaction he slowly passed,
as he too often did, to depreciation of himself. Dick might do so much to help the
great Cavendish; Dick was so sensible, so
prudent, so wise and good; all that he,
Fabian, was good for, was to exhort, to
entreat, to implore his friend not to abandon the great work. "I shall stay here,"
he said with great determination, "whether
you stay or go; but what can I do? I
know myself — none better; a sensitive

excitable creature; in a fever when I ought
to be cool. If I see the right thing, I do
the wrong thing; I trip at the critical
moment. Even now, if I had force, if I
could impose my will, I would weld you,
Dick, to this man, whom we have found
here, with his gigantic mind rusting in
this motionless corner; and you and he
together should—should move the world.
And instead of being strong to do this,
I am weak as water; I dash myself
against you like the wave on the rock.
Yes, you are a rock. When you and he
are together, instead of being able to weld,
I am myself shaken like a reed; I am all
nerves; I know him to be great and good;
I love you more than any one in the world;
and yet, when you are together, I feel your
cold mutual distrust in every nerve. Together you torture me—it's combinations
of people that torture sensitive creatures
—poor weak creatures; it's something to

know oneself a fool; good-night Dick—no
I can't stop, and I can't go with you—
good-night and God bless you." The last
words came back with a sort of sob from
the gallery, whence Fabian was already
dashing for the stairs.

It was not the first time that Dick had
seen Mr Deane under the influence of great
excitement. He followed him out of the
room, and he called " Good-night " after his
flying figure with a voice full of friendliness. Then he came back and looked with
a smile at Ossie, who was still sitting silent
on the portmanteau.

" Well, he's mad anyhow," said Ossie, as
if he derived some faint unholy consolation
from this belief.

" The first thing in the morning," said
Dick, " I shall look up Piero ; and as soon as
he can collect the men and beasts, we'll start."

" I don't think I shall go," said Ossie
ruffling his brows and pouting.

Dick thought that he was imitating an expression of Miss Holcroft, and turned shortly on his heel. "Good-night," he said.

At this hint Mr Langdon slowly rose from his humble seat. He stood first on one foot, then on the other. "Mind, I don't promise to go," he said.

"Piero shall come back for you, if you don't; but you'll come; you'll think better of it in the morning."

"No," said Ossic as sullenly as he could say it—"I shan't promise."

"Good-night," said Dick.

"Mind, I haven't promised," said Ossic from the gallery outside.

"You go to bed," said his cousin shortly, and he shut his door.

The next morning Dick was up betimes. He found Piero, and went with him in search of the other men. They could not start early, but Dick was determined that he would not sleep another night in Damascus.

When the necessary orders had been given and the preparations were going forward, he had leisure to think of his friends. He had little doubt but that both Fabian and Ossie would go with him; but he soon found that he was at least partly mistaken. He found Fabian at the door of the hotel, and he saw at once that he was very determined. Mr Deane look tired, as if he had spent a restless night; but his lips were tight set and his eyes sombre. He was silent and dark, as a volcano after an eruption. When Dick asked him his intentions, he answered briefly that he should stay where he was for the present, and that he would write to the care of the British Embassy at Therapia. Dick reminded him that their troop were to be dismissed at Beyrout, and offered to send Piero back to him; but he declined the dragoman; he was to be the guest of Mr Cavendish Tisley. There was clearly no room for argument. Dick asked where Ossie was, but Fabian had not seen him. Then he inquired for the Holcrofts, and learned with a momentary disappointment that they had gone away for the day with a consular friend. The next minute, however, he congratulated himself on not having to say good-bye. He charged Fabian to say all sorts of friendly things for him. By this time he was impatient to be on the road.

And now Dick's patience was sorely tried. He hunted high and low for his cousin, and could not find him. He began to think that he had hidden himself for love of mischief. At last the whole cavalcade appeared in the road — men and mules and asses—and with them Piero, alert upon his little horse, delighted to have people to direct once more, shouting, flourishing his whip, and wheeling in the dust. Then a few lazy Orientals squatting in the shadow of the house saw the young Englishman stamping in the sun, and wondered. Dick was on the point of sending the dragoman and his second in command to scour the city in different directions, when Ossie came lounging down the street with a cigarette in his mouth. In the distance he seemed to be smiling with great good humour; but as he drew near, he resumed a dejected air. However, he made no further objections to departure. Finding that all his goods were packed, he said that he supposed he had better go. Grumbling softly he allowed himself to be hoisted into the saddle.

"Good-bye, Fabian!" said Dick; "don't forget to write. And don't forget to say good-bye to the Holcrofts."

There was something in this last charge, which seemed to amuse Mr Langdon. He turned his head away, lest Dick should see that he was smiling.

"Good-bye," said Fabian gravely; and with jingling and jolting and strange cries the procession started.

A week later the cousins were on board a French steamer, which lay opposite to the widely-curved shore and white houses of Beyrout. They had dismissed the dragoman and the sub-dragoman and all their company; they had brought their luggage on board and inspected their clean airy cabins; and now they sat on the wide deck under the motionless awning, and gazed at the still blue water. Thus they would be doomed to sit for a week or more; for the steamer's progress was determined rather by freight than by passengers, and, as she lay now before Beyrout, so would she lie before Latakia, and Tripoli, and Alexandretta, lazily inquiring for goods.

Not even the prospect of this slow voyage disturbed the equanimity of Dick Hartland. As he could not make the boat go faster, he congratulated himself that he should get a glimpse of Rhodes, and of Smyrna ; but the chief reason of his content was that he had left Damascus behind him. Looking back on that ancient city he felt as if he had been dallying in Capua, growing lazy and cross, while events great enough to stir the blood of heroes were in progress in the world. "It seems as if we were to have this ship to ourselves," he said to Ossie, as he got up and went to the vessel's side. "No," he added ; "there's a boat coming."

"Is there ?" asked the other lazily and with his pretty innocent air.

"Yes. A man and a woman. Hullo ! By George !—Ossie !" Ossie came to his side.

"It's the Holcrofts," said Dick.

"Is it ?" asked Ossie after a pause.

Dick had been staring with all his eyes at the advancing boat ; but there was

something so strange in the excessive indifference of his cousin's question, that he
turned upon him in an instant. There was
no indifference in the tell-tale face; it was
radiant with suppressed glee.

"You knew it?" cried Dick, and the
question needed no answer. " Well, I—"
he began again, and then he began to
laugh. Then Mr Langdon permitted himself to laugh also.

CHAPTER XXXI.

AFTER all, the leisurely coasting voyage was very pleasant. Day after day the sea lay flat beneath the wide radiance of the sun, with scarce a ripple, and with scarce a cloud the curved expanse of heaven was deep and blue. Dick and Ossie and their American friends had the main deck to themselves; and there they sat all day under the widespread awning, reading or talking, or looking with a moment's interest at some object on the empty Asian shore. Almost before he had forgiven the Holcrofts for their presence, Dick was congratulating himself on it. He was ready to affirm that Mr Holcroft was the pleasantest travelling-

companion in the world, always interested
but never excited, ready but not eager to
talk, with a quiet humour and an indom-
itable sweetness of temper. As for his
daughter Kitty, Dick told himself that he
need have no fears about her ; that he had
only to keep an eye on his cousin. This
would be something to do ; and he liked
to have something to do. Very soon he
began to think that even this occupation
was unnecessary. It is true that the young
lady seemed well content that Ossie should
be often near her and should amuse her
with his intermittent talk ; but she was
apparently far more interested in her own
various occupations. She sketched with
remarkable industry, when the ship lay
motionless before some little town, which
furnished a sharp contrast of light and
shadow, a tower, a minaret, a palm-tree,
or little bits of bright colour, where the
natives lay or lounged on the low wall

by the sea. And when there was nothing to paint, she produced a volume of
the works of Goethe, and commanded Mr
Langdon not to talk. And one day, when
she was tired of reading, she appeared on
deck with a guitar; and it was only after
a full hour given to the most diligent prac-
tising of exercises that she consented to play
a little air, and to sing therewith a little
song, which she sang with a very sweet
fresh voice, and a simplicity which set
Dick wondering. He wondered if this
simplicity were not a form of consummate
artfulness, a superfine affectation. He wondered if women could be at once so clever
and so simple. This simplicity agreed well
enough with the frankness of her speech,
and the calm unabashed looks with which
she met the eyes of men ; but Dick found
it hard to reconcile this same simplicity
with her experiences of fashionable society,
and even more with her undoubted clever-

ness. He felt sure of her cleverness; she must have seen and heard so much of the world; how then could her simplicity be genuine? And yet he did not like to decide that she was affected. He wondered if women were not wholly different from men. Of course he had heard often enough that one must expect contradictory qualities in a woman; but he had always put this down as part of the nonsense that men talk about women. However, no man had ever puzzled him, as this girl puzzled him. He could not help wondering about her, though he often told himself that it was a ridiculous waste of time.

One evening after dinner when Mr Holcroft and Ossie were playing chess, Dick left them and went on deck. When he reached the upper air, he stood still amazed by the loveliness of this mid-May night. The moon was almost full; and it seemed to fill the world with such softness and

splendour, that it was hard to believe that
this was the same moon, which gleamed so
cold and pale from flying clouds in England
far away. Wide and tremulous the great
path of light lay on the dark silent sea;
and through the silence and the twilight
of the enchanted hour the ship travelled
steadily forward. It seemed in harmony
with the spirit of the time that the faint
notes of the guitar came softly to where
the young man stood. Dick went forward
with a slight laugh at his own feeling for
the beauty of the night. Whether she had
heard the laugh or obeyed the caprice of
the moment, Miss Holcroft received the
young man, who came between her and the
moonlight, with a reproachful look; and
her voice was almost petulant as she said,—
"I cannot play when you come; you par-
alyse me." Dick found nothing better to
say than that he was awfully sorry.
"Yes," she continued; "you are so critical."

"No, no," said he; "at least not too critical, I hope. I promise not to criticise your playing, if you will play for me."

"You are very observant; and very critical; and you——"

"Do play something."

"And you hate talking about yourself," she said, well pleased to give an unexpected ending to her sentence.

Dick laughed, but he felt himself flush; he felt that she was not far from the truth; she was certainly clever. "There are so many better things to talk about," he said lightly.

She looked up at him, as he leaned against the ship's side, but she could not see his face, which was in deep shadow. "Is that what you really think?" she asked. "I did not know that you were so humble."

"I hope I haven't been offensively arrogant—but you are making me talk about myself after all. How clever you are!"

"I wish I were clever," she said, looking across the sea with wide-open eyes. "It makes me so mad when men call women clever. They either mean that we have got some poor little accomplishments—like twanging the guitar for instance——"

"Do twang the guitar!" said Dick, as she paused.

"Or else it means that we are designing, and horrid," she continued.

Something in Dick's thoughts made him slow with an emphatic denial.

"Perhaps that is what you think of *me*," she said; she looked at him with the pouting lip and the pretty mutinous expression.

He was thinking at the moment that she looked like an elf in that strange light, so delicate fair and young; as if she might melt into the night, when the moon withdrew herself from the eyes of men; but for all her elfin charm her words jarred on him.

He did not like her to say such things.
He did not flatter himself that she spoke
more freely to him than to other men; and
he was not pleased to fancy her demand-
ing, what some other chance acquaintance
thought of her. Then he told himself that
it was no business of his; he asked himself why he should care how this girl spoke
to men; and as there was clearly no reason
to be found, he convinced himself that of
course he did not care.

Meanwhile Miss Holcroft seemed to have
forgotten that her last speech required an
indignant denial. She was looking across
the silent waveless sea, and humming softly
to herself. Presently she began to touch
the guitar again; and at last to a simple
accompaniment she began to sing low-
voiced a little German song. There seemed
to her only hearer a tenderness such as he
had never noticed in a song before.

" What does it mean ? " he asked, when

he had waited a little while in silence hoping for more, and no more came.

"I will sing it in English," she said; "a friend of mine translated it for me."

Dick wondered who this friend was, who could make verses for her. He had never made a verse in his life. Then the girl sang to the same soft accompaniment—

> Like to a perfect flower,
>   Pure, holy, fair thou art;
> I look on thee, and sadness
>   Sinks down into my heart.
>
> I feel that I must be laying
>   My hands upon thy hair,
> And praying God he would keep thee
>   So holy, pure, and fair.

She sang scarcely above her breath; it seemed as if she rather spoke than sang the words, but very sweetly and clearly. The softness of the wonderful night, the moonlight in the air and on the water, seemed to find a voice in the simple music. As Dick looked down on the girl, who her-

self looked so delicate flower - like in the
mysterious air, a strange tenderness possessed him.   He would like to guard this
lovely creature, who looked a child, from
all taint of worldliness.   He clean forgot
that but a few minutes before he had convinced himself that he did not care how
she spoke to men.   At the moment he
could almost have prayed, that she too
might keep the innocence and holiness of
childhood.   But for a sound instinct, he
too might have laid his hand upon that
soft brown hair.

At last Dick Hartland roused himself
from a mood unprecedented in his career.
He felt that he must say something to break
the absolute silence.   It was with a change
of tone, which was too abrupt, that he
asked — " Did your friend Goethe write
the verses ? "

"No," she said, " or I should not like
them so much.   I hate Goethe."   She

spoke the more strongly for his abruptness ;
she was quick to feel slight variations of
tone or manner. Dick laughed at her un-
compromising declaration. " How cynically
you laugh ! " she said.

" No, no," said Dick ; " nobody ever
called me cynical. I hate cynicism."

She looked seaward again and was silent
for a time. Then she said seriously, and
with a slow emphatic nod of her head,
" Some day you will discover that you
are profoundly cynical about women."

" Women ! women ! " said Dick ; " I
begin to think that women are the most
puzzling things in the world."

" Your friend Goethe made a study of
them," she said ; " and that's why I don't
like him. He did not mind hurting them,
if he amused himself ; and he talked about
improving himself. He looked down on
them, like stepping - stones in a stream ;
he went away dry-shod himself, and there

were they left behind, and—and he talked about self-culture, and it was nothing but flirtation." She laughed and nodded decisively, as if she triumphed in this neat conclusion to her little speech.

Dick laughed too. "I don't know much about Goethe," he said; "but don't you suppose there were two sides to the question?" This was a favourite phrase of Mr Hartland. "Perhaps these German girls——" he began again.

"No," she said, interrupting him; "it was flirtation. Are you a flirt Mr Hartland?"

This question came to the young man with a shock, which was extremely unpleasant. He said nothing, but he looked down darkly, as if he would try to read her face, which was uncertain in the growing dusk. Though he could not distinguish her expression, he had an instinctive belief that there was demure amusement in her eyes and mouth. He had very

seldom been laughed at; it seemed absurd
that this quick-witted young lady should
turn him into ridicule. So he answered
with his lightest manner, and reminded her
that she had found out how unwilling he
was to talk about himself. "Wasn't it
you," he asked, "who said that you had
come abroad to improve yourself? What
do young ladies mean by self-culture? Do
you gain much information from my cousin
Ossie for instance?"

"Mr Langdon is charming," she said
with a meditative air; "he is *very* un-
English."

"Thank you," said Dick. "Anyway I
am glad he persuaded you to come on to
Constantinople."

Miss Holcroft turned quickly to him.
"O Mr Hartland," she began, and then she
paused as if she were too astonished to go
on. "Do you really think," she said at
last, "that we followed you?" As he

hesitated, she went on quickly. "We had just heard," she said, "from our legation that it was safe to go to Constantinople, and we told your cousin that we were going; and then he told us that you were going too; and he said the prettiest things, and — O Mr Hartland, you have given yourself away. I had no idea of the vanity of Englishmen."

Dick felt that he had said the wrong thing. He did not see that there was anything offensive in his speech, but he felt that she saw it. Though she was half laughing as she spoke, she was a little indignant too. Dick made haste to remind her that at least he had not flattered himself, that he had anything to do with her decision; but Miss Holcroft seemed not to heed his words. She had risen, and was listening with the pretty head, of which by this time only the outline was visible, turned away from him.

"Kitty!" called Mr Holcroft, and his tall form appeared through the growing darkness. She went to her father.

"Good-night!" said Dick with great politeness.

"Good-night," she said with a little bow, as she took her father's arm.

"Good-night," cried Mr Holcroft pleasantly, as he was led away.

CHAPTER XXXII.

When Dick woke the next morning in his narrow bed, there was no sound of machinery in his ears, but only the voice of Mr Holcroft calling blithely in the passage. After a knock at the door the fresh clean-shaved face appeared, as the tall gentleman stooped in the doorway. "Hurry up," he said, "and come and coffee. The Captain goes ashore in less than an hour and has asked the pleasure of our company."

"All right," said Dick; "where are we?"

"At Rhodes," he answered, "in the shadow of the world-renowned Colossus."

It was with no expectation of seeing that long lost wonder of the world, that

Dick made haste to dress himself. He was thinking rather of the girl, who had sung in the moonlight; he was wondering in what mood he should find her. He felt a slight pleasurable excitement at the thought of seeing her again, and making his peace, as he was sure he should make it, easily enough.

Miss Holcroft was very quiet and demure. She sat very close to her father in the boat; she looked and listened, but scarcely spoke a word. Her father was in the gayest humour, as glad to go ashore as a midshipman on a holiday. It was a delightful morning, with all the freshness still in the air and a taste of the sea, though the hot sun was rising over the trees, and the shadows of the square white houses lay black upon the ground. But Mr Holcroft's pleasure did not reach its height till he came to the top of the famous Street of the Knights. There he stood still, and

after a time he waved one long arm, and
pointed, and looked at his companions.
"Why in thunder," he began slowly and
emphatically, "did nobody at home tell
me of this thing?" Though the question
was indignant, he smiled while he asked
it, and showed all his even white teeth.
"That is worth coming all the way to
see," he continued. "That street leads
straight into the Middle Ages; that is the
greatest street in the world."

As he looked round cheerfully for acquiescence, his daughter met his eye demurely
and murmured,—"Beacon Street?"

Mr Holcroft laughed aloud. "Well," he
said, "this is older;" and then possessed
by a happy thought, he added, "Sit right
down and make me a drawing."

She looked at him with pretended astonishment at his arbitrary tone, and then she
smiled too. "I must sketch it from the
other end," she said. So they walked down

the slope; and Dick, who had been carry-
ing the camp-stool and sketch-book, as a
sort of mute apology for his clumsy speech
of the evening before, placed them where he
was bidden. He was thinking what a perfect understanding there was between father
and daughter, and that she never looked so
pretty as when she looked at her father.
While he was thinking of something pleasant to say, Ossie slipped by his elbow and
bent over the sketch, which was already begun. At the same time Mr Holcroft, whose
interest in the place had by no means
abated, laid a long hand on Dick's shoulder,
and began to push him up the slope again,
pointing out to him with the same emphasis the unique charm of the street.
The street is steep and narrow, and on
either hand the dark Gothic buildings rise
continuous; and in one place an arch is
thrown across it, a mysterious passage-way
between two grim dwellings. On the old

brown walls the knightly coats of arms are
clear, as if they had been sharply chiselled
yesterday; for in that air the decay of stone
is slow, nor has the Turk desire of any
change. Indeed the only sign of Turkish rule are two or three light trellised
windows thrust through the sober walls.
"Those old knights might be in these
houses now," said Mr Holcroft beaming
on them impartially, and pressing Dick's
shoulder with his strong fingers; but at
the moment the young man's eyes had
wandered down the narrow street, to where
another young man leaned over a girl's
drawing with the sunshine on his hair.
For now the Eastern sun was charming
the ancient street from its sobriety; and
the sketcher found employment for her
swain by making him hold her large white
umbrella over her dainty head. In spite
of the just and emphatic observations of
Mr Holcroft, it is to be feared that the

peculiar charm of this old knightly street, so serious and dignified in an island full of brightness and blossom, was not more than half apparent to the eyes and mind of Mr Richard Hartland.

At last, after many wandering glances Dick looked once more, and saw that Miss Holcroft had left her place and was coming up the street, while Ossie stood alone by the empty camp-stool. As the girl came near, he saw that the faint rose of her cheek was heightened, and her eyes were bright. She put her hand on her father's arm, and for a moment leaned against his shoulder, as she put her sketch into his hand. Mr Holcroft looked at the little work critically; and then he passed it on to Dick without a word, but with a smile full of unhidden pride. Slight as it was, the little sketch had caught the spirit of the place; and the young man thought yet once again, how clever this girl was.

As they stood there together, and Ossie came towards the group with the camp-stool hanging from a listless hand, they were aware of a French sailor hurrying with much animation. He came to tell them that the captain had found no addition to his cargo, and was already getting up steam.

"Ask your captain to wait till I bring along this street. I shall take it home, and set it up on the Common." Mr Holcroft spoke gravely, but as he used his own language, the sailor only turned his brown face with inquiry and with eyes and ear-rings twinkling, and then with a courteous bow led the way to the boat.

It was in the evening of the same day, when they were steaming steadily forward over the dreaming sea, that Dick saw Ossie coming to him with an air most woe-begone. This long face always meant that Mr Langdon needed consolation; but now the smile, with which his cousin always met it, came less readily than usual. Ossie had come to confess a most unlucky error. As he was leaning over Miss Holcroft's sketch that morning, he had said something — better left unsaid ; and she had been much offended. Then Dick remembered the look of her face, as she had come to her father. Ossie also was offended—mightily offended. He could not understand it; the fatal something was absolutely nothing; it was too absurd of her to object to it. "It's the sort of thing," he said with a growing sense of injury, "that I've said to lots of girls ; and she was so jolly ; I never dreamt of her minding ; I've said that sort of thing to awfully nice girls who ain't a bit fast."

"I know you think you may say anything to women," said Dick severely.

"But this wasn't anything. I'll tell you what I said."

"I don't care what you said."

Ossie looked at his cousin pathetically.
"What did *she* say?" asked Dick after
a pause.

"Nothing. She just got up and went
away; and now she's awfully polite."

"It's probably all right."

"What do you mean by all right?"
asked Ossie in an injured tone.

"It's just as well that you shouldn't be
on such intimate terms with—with her."

"Do you mean that you don't think she's
a nice girl?"

"Certainly not," said Dick shortly; "of
course I mean nothing of the kind."

"Very well then——" began the other
slowly; but by this time Dick was possessed with his common sense of responsi-
bility for his cousin, and he made haste to
say what he thought he ought to say,
though he liked it very little.

"Of course a girl may be perfectly nice,"

he said, "and all that, and well behaved,
and yet be frivolous and flirtatious and—
and in fact—but of course it can't do *you*
any harm."

The speech was not a model of clearness,
but it seemed to convey a meaning to the
other young man, though he kept silence
for a time, and only bit his thumb.
At last he said with unusual decision,
"She ain't frivolous." Dick's short laugh
expressed a feeling that Mr Langdon
measured frivolity by a peculiar standard.
"She shocks you," said Ossie; "she does
it on purpose." Dick looked quickly and
keenly at his cousin, who continued not
without secret amusement,—"She told me
so; she said it was great fun to shock you.
She has taken no end of trouble to remem-
ber the slang of some Yankee college; and
that's why she says things are 'tony' and
that 'they take the cake,' and all that.
She says that you think that all girls

should be exactly like English girls. She says that you are insular—'just as insular as you can be' is what she says."

Dick was half amused and half annoyed. "Anyway you may leave me out of the question," he said; "and to-morrow morning you've got to apologise, and to mind what you say for the future."

"But I don't understand it. If an English girl was as jolly and friendly, one might say anything to her."

"She isn't English — and it doesn't matter whether you understand it or not."

"It's all very well for you; but just think of me. Think what a difference it makes to me."

"What do you mean?" asked Dick impatiently; "what can it really matter to you whether she snubs you a little or not?"

"I'm awfully hard hit," said Ossie gloomily.

Here was a most perplexing person. Even Dick, who was fortunate in a long and varied experience of his cousin, was amazed at this last declaration. Though he had observed a series of scenes which he took to be parts of a comedy of mild flirtation, he had had no fear of any serious complications. He had quietly made up his mind to keep an eye on Ossie, and to pull him up short if it should ever be necessary. And now under his watchful eye and unrestrained by his guiding hand the contradictory youth had taken the plunge, and was already in deep water. It was necessary to drag him out. Dick thought that he must take strong measures. He threatened to abandon the delinquent; "It's no business of mine," he said.

"No, I suppose not," said the other mournfully.

"I don't even pretend to know," continued Dick, "whether you are a free man; whether you are engaged to Miss Bond or not. What earthly right have you to go falling in love all over the place?"

Perhaps this question was scarcely consonant with the previous declaration of neutrality. Certain it is that, in spite of its indignant tone, Ossie seemed to take heart of grace from it.

"But I can't help it," he said plaintively.

"You ought to help it. It's preposterous to go falling in love with every girl you see."

"I know it's weak," acknowledged Ossie; "but I can't help it. You know I don't make any pretences." In this speech there was a slight flavour of satisfaction with his moral humility, which drove Dick to say with unnecessary vehemence that he devoutly wished that he would pretend to something. Ossie shook his head gravely:

"It's a great misfortune to be made like me," he said; "I don't pretend to strength, or pluck, or anything. I'm a poor creature, and I know it."

"You needn't be, if you didn't like," said Dick, who had heard this sort of thing some thousand times already; "it's all your confounded laziness."

But Ossie only shook his head again, and sighed deeply.

During the rest of their coasting voyage it was but natural that Dick should sometimes regard his cousin with much uneasiness; and yet for the most part he felt no great anxiety. He had a comfortable confidence in Ossie's gift of falling on his legs, and in the ease of his changes. He thought it likely that they would meet some European ladies at Pera; and, if there were none of these, he thought that Mr Langdon's fancy would be safely diverted by some veiled and happily unapproachable beauty

of Stamboul.   As for Miss Holcroft, Dick
felt more and more strongly that she would
take care of herself.   He was glad that
she knew how to keep Ossie within bounds.
Every day he placed more confidence in
the theory, that she regarded young men
as created for the amusement of her idle
hours; while her serious interest was re-
served for the improvement of herself.
She read her German books, she played on
her guitar, she made many sketches; and
these young men might look or listen, if
they wished.   If she so thoroughly forgot
Ossie's indiscretion, that she was ready to
laugh with him, and perhaps at him a little,
she treated Dick more seriously.   She asked
him questions about England, and about
English poets and painters, of whom she
seemed to know more than he.   He began
to think that a friendship with a clever
girl was one of the pleasantest things in

life; he almost forgot those looks of hers
which had perplexed him in the first days.
And now the golden hours on the summer
sea were soon to be of the past. The travellers were borne by islands of exquisite clear
outline and soft splendid colour—islands
which, as the sun sank into the illumined
water, seemed almost transparent, pale, lum-
inous, violet beside the glow. At Smyrna
they were obliged to say good-bye to the
ship, in which they had enjoyed so prosperous a voyage, and to go on board of another
and a larger steamer, which had already
many passengers. And so the peculiar
charm was gone, and they all looked forward
to the end. And one morning they awoke,
and found the steamer at rest; and when
they met on deck, there were roofs and
slender minarets close to them, the ancient
cypresses of the Seraglio gardens, and the
dome of Saint Sophia eminent in the cool

clear light of dawn. There close beside
them in the centre of the ancient city big
ships lay on the deep silent waters of the
Golden Horn, and the sharp-pointed light
caiques ruffled the quiet surface as they
darted here and there.

CHAPTER XXXIII.

IT was very hot in Constantinople, hotter perhaps in the European hotels of Pera than in the dark narrow alleys of Stamboul. The travellers were eager to leave the city and go in search of the cool breezes of the Bosphorus. After the first great sight of the place from shipboard the visiting of mosques and treasuries seemed tame enough ; and when they had peeped into the lovely Mosque of St Sophia, which was but just purified from fevers and fever-stricken fugitives, they would have gone at once, had not Mr Holcroft displayed an unexpected interest in military matters. He was the more bent on visiting the Turkish

troops, who were busily strengthening their
positions around the city, because among
the letters which he carried there was one
to an officer who held an important command. Armed with this he was confident
that he would ride through the Turkish
lines as freely as if he were the Sultan,
and he asked Dick and Ossie to accompany
him as a picked body-guard. So it was
agreed that they should delay their departure for Buyuk Dere, which they had
chosen as their resting-place on the Bosphorus, for at least a day.

As they were riding up the open downs,
Mr Holcroft began to exhibit unusual excitement. He expressed unbounded admiration for the soldiers whom they met—
the short Turkish regulars, with honest
faces of a brick-dust colour, and broad
square shoulders which seemed built to
carry cannon. He pointed to them with a
beaming countenance as examples of what

men could be, who never saw money and
were paid for their fighting with a handful of rice; and when he smiled upon
them, they grinned at him with a childlike simplicity. Indeed so simple is the
nature of the Turk, while he has not
a penny, and so friendly was the appearance of the American, that all the sentries
after a brief colloquy with their Greek
guide, who combined astounding volubility
with prompt invention, allowed the travellers to pass. Thus it happened that after
riding for some miles over open downs—as
open and familiar as the downs of Sussex—
they came to the very key of the Turkish
position, where under a screen of inter-
woven boughs the generals were holding a
council of war; and on the very next line
of hills, white specks against the sky, were
Russian tents. Mr Holcroft grasped the
situation in a moment. He began eagerly
to point out how strong was this Turkish

position; how easily on the other hand
the Russians, if they wished, might break
the truce and bring on a battle as if by
accident; how much harder they would
find the capture of the city, than they
would have found it a month ago. He
was in the full tide of explanation, when
he was interrupted by the approach of the
officer, to whom the guide had carried the
letter of introduction. Polite as he was,
the distinguished soldier could not help
showing that he was by no means pleased
to see them there. He shrugged his shoulders, as he spoke of the sentries; and he
gave Mr Holcroft so cordial an invitation
to visit him on the next day at his head-
quarters, which were a mile or two nearer
the city, that it was abundantly clear that
he would make no effort to detain them
at the present time. So after mutual
apologies the travellers turned their horses'
heads eastward, and the officer after re-

peating his invitation to the American, returned to his consultation under the woven branches.

As they rode homeward, Dick expressed his surprise at Mr Holcroft's knowledge of military affairs; but he was a good deal more surprised to learn that the American had himself seen service.

"You had not heard of our war perhaps?" asked Mr Holcroft politely. Dick resented the imputation; but he could not help saying in answer that he had also heard of a transatlantic fondness for military titles.

"Many of us dropped them," said Mr Holcroft gravely, "when the fighting was done. For my part," he continued more gaily, "I had had more than enough. I did not like it; but it's a great country and worth fighting for—in spite of the politicians and the taxes. When you visit me in Beacon Street, you will see a picture of me in full uniform, and with half a horse. It was done to gratify the feminine vanity of my little girl. It is said to be simply splendid; it bears a striking resemblance to Prince Joachim Murat." When they had ridden a little farther—"I take it you think me a bad American," he said; "but I am not. I trust the sense of our people, when they care enough. When they commence to care about a thing, that thing has got to be put right. As to politicians, I don't know that ours are much worse than other people's. I expect you wouldn't find better fellows than these Turkish soldiers; but their Pashas would sell them, and each other, and the Mosque of St Sophia, and throw the Sultan in for nothing. And over yonder at San Stephano there must be many stolid fellows ready to die for their Slavonic kinsmen or their holy Czar; but I take it that their generals are pocketing the forage money, and that their diplomatists are scheming for each other's shoes, as well as for the finest harbour in the world."

"Of course there's right on both sides," said Dick, "and wrong too. I don't love the Russians as a lot; but after all they move, and the others can't; it's the difference between a future and a past—between life and death."

"You desperate young Britons," said Mr Holcroft smiling, "must have life in some shape."

"Dick goes in tremendously for politics," observed Ossie, who was tired of silence.

The American turned in his saddle and regarded Dick with friendly interest. "If you must have them," he said, "I hope you will take them lightly; and that they won't leave any bad after-effects."

They left their horses at the point of the Golden Horn; and then reclining in the light *caique* they sped quickly down the

great curve of the majestic harbour; and
they went ashore at the long rickety bridge
of boats, whereon all day the most varied
population in the world pass, most of them
for no reason, from Stamboul to Pera and
from Pera to Stamboul. There is always a
crowd on the bridge, and there may be seen
every colour, which nature and weather can
paint on the human countenance, or dye
and time give to the multiform clothing of
mankind. Mr Holcroft could never see
this bridge without stopping to look and
to moralise; and he only turned from it
now, when he found that he was pointing
out its superiority to all other bridges for
the sole benefit of a couple of swarthy Bul-
garian porters. Then he smiled broadly
upon this stolid audience, and followed
Dick and Ossic up the steep street of
Pera.

As they came under the shadow of the
hotel, a rose fell at their feet, and looking

up they saw Miss Holcroft in the balcony.
Dick's first thought was that the action
was pretty and the girl charming; but the
next moment he was accusing her of having
planned this pretty greeting, of assuming
an attractive attitude. He did not like
her to show herself to the open street; it
seemed bold, and excited in him a moment's
admiration of the veils and mufflers of the
East. And yet when this young lady of
the West came to meet them with all her
confidence and modesty, the young Englishman's little criticisms lay down and died
before her natural charm. He clean forgot
that he had ever been critical, and he was
only eager to please. And so in obedience
to a just instinct he began to speak of her
father, and to express his surprise again
that he had fought, and had never mentioned it.

"And you didn't know it!" she ex-
claimed—"why, he fought splendidly. I

must show you the account of his great charge."

"Kitty!" said Mr Holcroft; but his daughter shook her head at him. "You would like to see it, wouldn't you?" she said to Dick.

"I should like to see it awfully," said Dick who found himself staring at her. Indeed he was delighted with her beauty and her sweet natural enthusiasm.

"I have often told her," said Mr Holcroft sadly, "that I did not charge alone. There were a number of other persons implicated."

"They never would have gone without *you*," she said with her little chin in air and her eyes sparkling.

"If they had gone without me," he remarked slowly, "I expect that I should have been drummed out, and should have been sent home in disgrace."

"Don't, papa," she cried imperiously.

Then with both hands on her father's arm
as if she would control the tall gentleman
by force, with her delicate face flushed with
admiration of him, and her eyes still raised
to his, she said to Dick—"Isn't he perfectly horrid? He never will be serious;
but he can't help being a hero."

"Kitty! Oh!" The second exclamation
was much sharper than the first, for his
daughter had pinched the arm to which
she clung.

"Did you ever see such a little tyrant?"
asked Mr Holcroft with a voice full of love
and pride. This question was directed
to Dick, but for a moment he forgot to
answer. He was seldom so unready. When
it was time to go, he forgot to drop
her hand as quickly as usual; and again
and again that evening there came back to
him a memory of her sweet serious eyes.
Nor did this strange effect pass with the
passing hour. During the whole of the

next day Dick Hartland was in a thoughtful mood, and Mr Osbert Langdon yawned
often in his company.

It was agreed that Mr Holcroft should
ride alone to make his visit at Head-
quarters; and that his English friends
should go up the Bosphorus on one of the
little steamers, and should secure rooms at
Buyuk Dere for themselves, and for the
Holcrofts who would follow them on the
next morning. So the two friends made
their little journey in the cool of the
evening, and engaged the necessary rooms;
and, when Ossie had fallen asleep after
dinner, Dick sat by the open window and
allowed his thoughts to wander in a very
idle manner. But for all their liberty his
thoughts would not wander far; they
returned wilfully to one object. It was
a night of stars and of lights far below
upon the waters, and of shadowy sweet
coasts, which made the watcher wonder

if they could be half so beautiful under the morrow's sun. Perhaps it was the influence of the place and of the hour, which made the energetic young Englishman so dreamy. The perfume of unseen roses came in to him; they reminded him of the girl who would come on the morrow. He thought of the soft brown hair; of the grave eyes which he had seen when he held her hand at parting; of the pouting of the lips with their arch defiance, which he had noticed so often. It was strange how clearly he could see this girl's face, though it was miles away. He leaned his cheek against his arm and gave himself to dreaming; he smiled into the dusk not knowing that he smiled; nor did he wake from his unusual reverie, until he found his lips murmuring a name. Then he stood up with a warm blush on his boyish cheek, and began to laugh at himself. "What's this?" he asked; "what's coming to me? It's all nonsense; this comes of mooning at a window"—and he laughed again. And then he leaned out once more into the fragrant night; and just to show that he dared to play with these idle fancies, which of course meant nothing, he whispered the name again as tenderly as he could. "Kitty," he whispered; it was a comical little name, he thought, when spoken sentimentally.

CHAPTER XXXIV.

DICK woke on the next morning with
a feeling of expectation which he could
not explain. When it suddenly occurred
to him that all this was because a girl
was coming, whom he had not seen for a
day, he laughed aloud at his folly. It
seemed absurd that he of all men should
be so dependent on his friends; but then
he reminded himself that he was far from
home and in a strange land ; this seemed
a good enough explanation, or at least
good enough to last till breakfast was
done. To breakfast Ossie came yawning,
and after fortifying himself with coffee
expressed an intention of dropping down

to Pera and telling the Holcrofts that
their rooms were ready. He set up this
resolution for Dick to knock down, and
he was faintly disappointed when it was
met with the advice to go before the sun
grew hot. At this he probably would
have abandoned the design, had not his
friend announced that he should accompany him as far as Therapia and ask at
the Embassy for letters. Thereupon, as
he did not feel energetic enough for opposition, he allowed himself to be started.

When Dick had returned with his letters,
he carried them to the window-seat, where
he had sat the night before ; but, when he
was there, he forgot to read, for he found
there the same thoughts, which had half
pleased and half perplexed him in the
evening. The place and the very attitude,
in which he leaned upon the striped divan,
seemed to recall the fancies, which he had
put away with laughter. Even when he

had opened his letters, he read some sentences twice or thrice with small understanding, and his eyes would wander to the outer air. Close to him, wreathed about the light balcony, great yellow roses were liberal in the light; and the awning, which fell almost to touch them, was petulant in the fickle air, which seemed to touch Dick's eyes and lips with a caress. Below him was a garden of more roses and sweet shrubs; and beyond that and far below he could see the water ruffled now and then by a light breeze, and in the pauses oily calm. With a great swing this way and a back swing that, the Bosphorus sweeps down from the Black Sea like a strong river; and there was small progress to be made against it with the fickle breeze of that morning. In the bays close under either shore ships from all lands lay idle; and only one was moving slowly with all sail set against the heavy stream.

Now, though Dick's eyes would wander to the light without and his thoughts stray from the reading, the letters, which he had found at Therapia, were not without interest. First he opened his mother's, and read it in leisurely fashion, pleasing himself in the intervals of his day-dream with her good report of all things at home. When he reached the postscript, he was roused to a keener interest; for in the postscript she had compressed the important news that Mr Kirby was to contest a county at the next election, and was most anxious that his young cousin should come home, and look after Redgate. Dick turned from his mother's neat characters to the boldly straggling direction of his more eminent relative. Mr Kirby had written his letter in the House of Commons, while he was waiting for a division; a few of his weighty, yet familiar sentences covered the ample sheet. He enjoined secrecy, and named his county. Then he wrote that of course Dick ought to succeed him at Redgate; that his own popularity with the town and the Hartland influence ought to make it a certainty; that in these days however nothing was safe without nursing; that Dick should come back at once and nurse the borough. Dick's first feeling was that the borough might wait, that there were better things in life than boroughs. He was smiling, as he put the letter in his pocket for future consideration; and he smiled with a livelier expectation as he opened the third epistle. This had been written by Fabian Deane within two days after his parting from his friends at Damascus; it is even probable that it had travelled in the same boat which had carried them to Smyrna; if so, it is almost strange that it had not made its presence felt,—so explosive were its contents. Some forty fleeting hours had produced a revolution; and Mr Cavendish

Tisley, who had been the force to move the Eastern world, was now described in terms which would have libelled the initiative of a feather-bed.

"Not another night," wrote Fabian, "will I spend under this impostor's sham-Mauresque roof. He is the Arch Impostor; a wind-bag blown up with conceit and old phrases; a bloated centipede, with fifty legs going each way; silent as a mummy and as likely to do anything useful; a self-important pudding. I wish I could describe him, but the fellow is such a humbug that he beggars description; and what he does crawling between heaven and earth is more than I can make out, unless he is spared for the sake of his good little Episcopal-close wife, who actually makes herself believe in this fantastic stuffed target, whom the poor little dear must have sworn to love and to obey! Talking of which, where are the Holcrofts? And when shall you be in

England? Write to me there, for I am going home by the shortest possible way and *must* find something to do. 'Must' is the word! Contemplation of this monstrous C. T. has made useful activity the first necessity of life. Come home too like the wise boy you always were!—Yours as ever, FABIAN DEANE."

"Talking of which, where are the Holcrofts?" said Dick to himself, as he folded his friend's letter. Nothing else in the letter had surprised him. He saw nothing unprecedented in Mr Deane's rapid flight from profound veneration to absolute contempt; and it seemed quite natural that no reason should be given for the change. For his own part he had decided long ago that little was to be gained from Mr Cavendish Tisley ; and the sight of Russian officers walking the streets of Pera in conspicuous uniforms had brought home to

him the very unsettled condition of the
Turkish empire so vividly, that he had
postponed all question of buying land in
Palestine till such time as man might
know, what power would be responsible for
order there. " Talking of which, where
are the Holcrofts ? " Dick repeated to himself. That was the sentence which struck
him. "Talking of what ? " he asked himself. " Come home too like the wise boy
you always were ! " What did he mean ?
Why was it wise to go home just now ?
He was rather annoyed with Fabian for
not being more explicit. He laughed as he
thought that his friend had spoken plainly
enough about the unfortunate Cavendish ;
but though he laughed, he was rather vexed.
The suggestion of going home made him
look again at his mother's letter ; and now
he seemed to read between the lines a constant wish that he would come home to her.
She had been careful never to urge him to

return, since he went away; and it was
hard to tell why this last letter seemed to
breathe a different spirit. She had written
that Mr Kirby said that he ought to come
back to the Borough; but as he read, he
felt that a stronger influence was on him
than that of Mr Kirby, or his Borough. If
he did go home now, it would be for his
mother's sake. He told himself that there
was no other reason, which should make
him put a sudden end to his wandering.
At least there was no immediate hurry;
he would take time to decide; this was
only wise. Besides he should like to know
what these other people were going to do.
"Talking of which, where are the Holcrofts?" Dick said to himself that there
was nobody like Fabian for finding a mare's
nest. He got up, and stood in the open window drumming on the pane with impatient
fingers. The door opened behind him.
Without doubt here they were; here were

the Holcrofts. He turned to greet them
with a face bright with welcome; but
there was nobody but Ossie—and Ossie in
his most melancholy mood.

"Where are they?" asked Dick.

"They ain't coming," answered Ossie re-
sentfully.

"Not coming! Why not?"

"You needn't abuse me about it. It isn't
my fault."

"But what did she say? Didn't she
give any reason?" It is worthy of note
that it did not occur at any moment to
either young man, that the change of plans
might have been due to Mr Holcroft.

"No," said Ossie; "she didn't give any
reason. She was just as jolly as usual.
She said she hadn't half done the Bazaar;
and that she couldn't live without shop-
ping. She wanted me to tell you particularly that she couldn't live without shop-
ping. I suppose you've offended her about

something." He paused for an answer, but, as Dick said nothing, he continued—" She said that in America girls didn't follow young men; she looked most awfully cheeky as she said it; she's the jolliest girl I ever saw ; I suppose there's nothing to do here; it seems a dull sort of place."

Dick was looking down to the waters of the Bosphorus and the steep shore opposite; and he seemed in no hurry to defend it from the charge of dulness. Somehow its beauty had gone, and left only its loneliness. There was no sound in the hot air ; the one ship, which had been trying to move against the stream, had given up the effort and dropped anchor under the shelter of the shore. Dick remembered that unlucky speech of his, in which he had seemed to imply that her presence on board the French boat was in some way due to theirs. This declaration of hers about American girls showed that she had not forgotten it.

He supposed that this trick, which she had played them, delighted her as a little piece of vengeance. Of course she expected them to appear penitent on the morrow; she wanted this petty proof of her power; after all she was no more than a spoiled child, capricious and vain ; after all she was nothing better than a little flirt.

Dick's meditations were interrupted by his cousin, who had dropped into that comfortable chair in which he had slept away some hours of the previous evening.

" I can't make out why you ain't awfully in love with her," said Ossie. Dick did not turn ; he stared straight out into the sunlight, but he felt the blood tingling in his ears. "She don't care a button for me—worse luck !" said Ossie a little later.

" Nor for me," said Dick shortly; "don't talk such nonsense."

Mr Langdon, who was regarding his own boots with tender interest, began to hum.

"Dickie," he observed at last more cheerfully, "you are a clod; you've no heart; you never had any."

"That's all right."

"If I were you, I would marry this girl to-morrow."

"And what reason have you to suppose, you blooming idiot, that she would look at me?" Though this question was unmistakably directed at the gentleman in the arm-chair, Dick still looked out of the window intently as if he were watching a procession.

"My dear Dick," said Ossie with temper unruffled by hard names, and his best air of worldly wisdom, — "My dear Dickie, she knows all about you."

"Oh does she!"

"Of course she does. She has asked me hundreds of questions about you, and your position, and your property, and all that."

"Oh!"

"Don't you know that all these American girls are dying to marry Englishmen with good position. Position—that's what they care about—and a park. Parks are the things for these American girls."

"Oh shut up," said Dick; "and don't talk such washed-out old nonsense."

"It's true," said Ossie wagging his head sagely; "everybody knows this sort of thing but you, and you're an old goose. You'll be caught some day and cooked. You're not the sort of chap that women refuse."

"Oh I know that stuff of yours," said Dick; but somehow this time he did not laugh at his cousin's worldly wisdom. He spoke crossly. The truth is that he was more out of humour with his pleasant world than he had ever been in his life before.

"Do you think of staying long in this lively spot?" asked Ossie presently.

"No," said Dick; "I think I shall have to go home."

"Go home!"

"Yes." He tossed Mr Kirby's letter to his cousin. "Redgate wants to be nursed," he said, and walked out of the room. He wanted to be alone.

CHAPTER XXXV.

DICK retired into solitude that he might consider his feelings; and so little accustomed was he to self-examination, that it was with a sense of solemnity little short of awe that he withdrew himself from his volatile cousin. He knew that the time had come when he must consider his position. He wondered how he had been content to drift so long. However, he would waste no more time in wonder; he must look this thing fairly in the face, and have done with it for ever. As he reviewed his thoughts and feelings of the last few weeks, he was ashamed of himself. He, who was in the habit of understanding

people so easily, had spent hour after idle
hour in questioning and doubting about a
girl. He, who had always seen so clearly
the relative importance of the facts of life,
had been dwelling on trifles lighter than
air, considering the meaning of a look or
a careless word. He had been puzzled,
perplexed, out of temper. As he looked
back on his strange moods, he exaggerated
his irritability ; for so sweet was Dick
Hartland's natural temper, that his occasional crossness seemed monstrous in his
eyes. As he recalled his feelings, he told
himself again with greater emphasis that a
continuation of this state of things would
be intolerable. He asked himself what was
the meaning of this doubt, and perplexity,
and irritation. Was it possible that they
were the first symptoms of that unknown
malady of Love? If so, it was strange
that his feeling for this girl was so like
annoyance. Did his friends think that he

was in danger of falling in love, and was it
that strange thought which had prompted
Fabian Deane's question about the Holcrofts,
and Ossie's careless remarks—perhaps even
caused the spirit of his mother's letter?
Was he really in danger of falling in love?
To that important question had he come at
last.   He stopped in his solitary walking
and squared his shoulders as if he would
emphatically answer, No; but even then
the little word was not uttered.   He
wished to be exactly true with himself;
and this girl still puzzled him so much,
that it was hard to be certain of the
exact truth.

As Dick walked backward and forward,
he gradually found more and more comfort
in one thought, which seemed to promise
him a firm ground for action.   This thought
had not a heroic air, for it was a thought
of flight.   It seemed certain to him that he
had better put an end to all this question-

ing and unworthy splitting of straws by
promptly removing himself from the atmosphere which caused them.   If there were
really the remotest chance of his becoming
a victim of the tender passion, the reasons
for flight were twice as strong.   Had he
not declared to himself that when he chose
a wife, he would give weight to all his
mother's prejudices; that this should be a
sort of atonement for his obstinacy about .
the land?   As for Miss Holcroft, he told
himself with a touch of bitterness that, if
he were certain of nothing else in this
matter, he was certain at least that she
did not love him.   He laughed at the
thought.

As Dick went through again the few
short weeks since first he saw the girl, who
had so unduly occupied his thoughts, it
seemed to him that almost from the first
he had had two pictures of her in his
mind, and had been hesitating between

them. The one picture represented a girl
transparently honest for all her cleverness;
with quick feelings but a high standard of
conduct; with a serious interest in all
forms of art as means for her improvement, and yet not contemptuous of such
pretty decorations of life as dress or pleasant talk of the trifles of every day.
The other picture was of a less amiable
character. It represented one who was
not honest; whose frank looks and manners were assumed for a purpose—put on
with care like her gowns and gloves;
whose good conduct was due to calcula-
tion and cool blood; who cultivated music
and painting as accomplishments which
added to her power of attraction; who
found the chief business of life in amusing herself, and the greatest amusement
in flirtation. Dick now declared to himself, that doubt as to which of these two
pictures was the true representation of

the original was the cause of all his perplexity.

Dick presently returned to the belief, of which he had now laid firm hold, that, whether Miss Holcroft resembled the better portrait or the worse, she did not care for him. If she were the true straightforward girl, in whom at some moments he had felt such confidence, it was still certain that her interest in him was as nothing in comparison with her interest in her own improvement. She was still comically unlike that ideal gentle wife, whom he had purposed to wed some day for the satisfaction of his mother, and for the providing of a quiet element in his own busy useful life—of whom he had dreamed, now as of a haven of rest, now as of a dim grey-clad angel whose pleasure and duty it was to smoothe the wrinkles from his brow. If Miss Holcroft were honest and true, she was still far from her whom he

would do well to marry; and luckily it
was certain that she did not care for him.
If on the other hand she were no more
than a clever comedian of real life, who
lived for these little comedies of two idle
players, it was certain that he was no more
to her, than a player in a theatrical episode,
a name on a list of men, a page in her
album of photographs.

As Dick grew more and more impatient
of this necessary consideration of his position, immediate departure seemed more and
more clearly to be the solution of all difficulties. If the girl was true, Dick felt
certain that she would marry no man
whom she did not really love; and so he
had better go, while he could go without
pain. If she were no better than a little
flirt, the reasons for flight were terribly
strong; for such a girl, though she did
not love him, might marry any man for
position—for the park, which Ossie had

talked about. It was only too clear what
Ossie thought of her in spite of all his
admiration. Dick in his eagerness for
certainty was inclined to take the final
leap; to admit that this girl was no more
than the little frivolous American flirt, of
whom he had heard, and that his occasional
belief in her higher qualities was due to his
inexperience of the species, and to her uncommon cleverness. All the arguments
seemed to be on that side. How could her
air of frankness be genuine after seasons of
frivolous society? Would so unsuspicious a
person as himself ever have doubted her at
all, if her nature had been so simply true?
He said to himself that she had been playing with him, as she had been playing with
Ossie. It was time for flight, and he would
go; and he would take his cousin with him.

When Dick had made up his mind to go,
he spent but little time in settling details.
He decided to return to Pera on the next

morning, and there to secure berths on the
steamer which left on the following day.
Meanwhile being by this time heartily sick
of mental discussion he determined to do
something energetic before sundown. He
thought that a brisk ride would clear his
head of idle thoughts; he knew that his
host had horses; he was unwilling to
leave the Bosphorus without one peep at
the forest of Belgrade, which was so close
at hand. So first he ordered that two
animals should be saddled at once; and
then he went to tell his cousin all that
was before him. He had made plans for
Ossie, as well as for himself; it seemed
like old times; and the pleasantest thing
about this necessary retreat was that it
would restore his friend to his care. Dick
never doubted that Ossie would accept his
decision, and would forget the Holcrofts,
father and daughter, almost before he
was out of sight of land. Since they had

first seen the girl, faint shadows of distrust had come between them; there had been another influence on the wayward youth. Now Dick warmed his heart with the thought that he would carry his cousin unscathed away; that he would put things right for him at home in England; that the old frank comradeship would be restored with all its charm. So it was with a smile on his lips that he told Ossie of his plans; and Ossie so far justified his expectations that he made no objection. Indeed he said nothing audible; but, as he began to prepare himself for the afternoon's ride, it was clear that he acquiesced in that arrangement at least.

Out they rode in the pleasant drowsy air of the summer afternoon; and as they rode, there opened before them a country familiar to their eyes as Surrey, swelling into gentle hills, rich and warm, with here and there a patch of growing wheat. They clattered along the white road, and Dick's spirits rose with the movement. Riding fast they were soon in the skirts of the forest; and there under the cool shadows their pace became slower and slower. And this woodland too was familiar enough, with its oaks and its poplars, its deep fern freckled with broken lights. Thoughts of home and of the coverts of Claring came to Dick; and his eyes peered eagerly through the dark cool screen beside him. Beyond this first dark screen the forest sloped downward, and the trees on the edge of the slope caught the full sunlight, and somewhere there an unseen nightingale made the summer air one music with the throbbing of his song. Perhaps the young man's review of his feelings had left them somewhat tender; he had never before been so keenly affected by such little gifts of Nature, as this sunlight which penetrated the wood a little way away, as this bird that sang in a bush. His horse moved slowly under him; he forgot his dear companion; for a moment in the near shadows he had a vision of an arch innocent face, which looked so little guileful; but in a moment too he had brushed it away with decision. To put an end to such fancies he turned to his silent comrade; and then he saw for the first time sticking out between two buttons of Ossie's coat the butt end of the pistol, which he had insisted on bringing from England. "What on earth do you bring that thing for?" asked Dick.

"Good men are scarce," said Ossie; "I'm bound to take care of myself. 'Sauve qui peut!' you know."

Dick laughed, and pushed the old horse forward. When he had gone a little farther, it occurred to him that the shadows of the trees would be long on the ground, if the path were not so narrow; it must be time to go back. He turned his horse, and then

it struck him that he was a little doubtful about the way. They had turned off
the road, and now, when they wished to
regain it, they almost immediately came to
a place where two paths crossed, and there
they paused uncertain. Dick declared for
one way, Ossie for the other.

"I'll go down this, and see," said Ossie.

"All right," said Dick; "only don't get
out of shouting distance."

Dick's path brought him in a very few
minutes to the right road; but as he rode
out from the darkness of the trees, he saw
something, which half inclined him to seek
shelter again. Not more than two hundred
yards distant and coming to meet him was
a small body of foot-soldiers. They were
straggling down the road with no officer
to be distinguished; all alike looked dirty
and reckless. It was probable that they
belonged to that part of the Turkish army,
which had been placed to guard the head

of the Bosphorus; but they were wholly
unlike the stalwart honest men whom Dick
had seen on the downs above Constantinople. At a glance Dick pronounced them
an ill-looking lot. It flashed across him
that they might take him for a Russian
wandering about during the armistice;
that, whether they took him for a Russian
or no, these were the sort of fellows whom
a solitary man in a lonely place and in the
growing darkness of the wood might tempt
to plunder, if not to snap of pistol. The
thought of a pistol brought Ossie's weapon
to his mind; so far as he could see, these
rascals had no rifles with them; they looked
like sorry rascals indeed, and if there were
a row, the sight of a second horseman with
a revolver would cow them in a moment.
As soon as he had come out of the trees, he
knew that he was seen; and as he remembered his cousin, he shouted his name
loudly, and rode slowly forward with an

air of carelessness. Almost as he shouted,
he saw Ossie break from the wood beyond
the straggling soldiers, who turned to
look at him. "Ossie!" shouted Dick;
but Ossie seemed to be in difficulties
with his horse, pulling his head about
and spurring him in an angry manner;
and the horse, with a great noise on the
hard road, galloped away towards Buyuk
Dere. Dick felt a moment's regret, for he
was sure that if his cousin had come to
meet him with his pistol carelessly displayed, this rabble, which separated them,
would have been tame enough. He had
time to think it strange that Ossie had
not even glanced down the road; he supposed that all his attention was given to
his beast, and that the galloping hoofs
must have drowned his shout. As it was,
there was probably nothing to fear. He
kicked the old grey into a canter. As he
quickened his pace, he saw that the strag-

glers spread themselves with seeming carelessness across the road. "God help me!"
he said .below his breath; and then he set
his teeth. Within a few yards of the soldiers he suddenly tightened his rein and
his knees and gave his beast a smart cut
with his whip; the good old horse sprang
forward; there was a shout around him,
and a dingy half - bred ruffian caught his
rein, and swung forward on the road
beside him. And now Dick's blood was
dancing, and with a short sharp crack he
brought his heavy-headed whip down on
the dusky wrist, and his horse galloped
free. He heard the rascal's howl, and he
gave a great shout in answer, as he bent
low, expecting every instant the whistle of
a pistol ball. However nothing came; and
as he pulled up and looked back, he laughed
at himself. It was not half an adventure.
He had never been aggressive; and yet the
blood was tingling in his veins; some old

fighting spirit was eager in his heart; he was half inclined to go back and ride through them again. Then again he laughed at himself for his folly, and patted the old grey's neck and set him in motion towards his home.

As Dick drew near to Buyuk Dere, he saw Ossie riding back to meet him. Ossie was very white, and as soon as he was within speaking distance he began asking questions with a hurried and excited manner.

"I've had a little adventure all to myself," said Dick in his triumphant mood, as soon as he could get in a word; "I shouted to you; didn't you hear me shout?"

"No," said Ossie in a moment; Dick looked at him with a sudden fear; a feeling of sickness came over him, as he knew that Ossie had lied.

CHAPTER XXXVI.

NIGHT brought little comfort to Dick Hartland. He was in a mood of such bitterness, as he had never known,—as he would have maintained to be impossible for him. He had been contemptuous with easy good nature of all railing against life and the world; but now life seemed poisoned, and the world a base world, in which no woman was worthy of love, no man capable of friendship. He asked no explanation from Ossie, nor did he meet him with rebuke. Neither explanation nor rebuke could do any good. The only scrap of comfort came to him, when his cousin told him that he did not wish to start for England at once. A friendly *attaché* had offered him a room at Therapia, and he should like to go there for a week or two. Though Ossie's manner was unusually submissive, Dick made no effort to dissuade him; he was eager to get away from him for a time. The cousins were uncomfortable together, and they were both glad when the parting was over.

As soon as Dick had set foot in Pera, he went to engage a cabin on the ship which was to start on the evening of the next day. Then he wrote a note to Miss Holcroft, and asked at what time next morning he might come to say good-bye to her and to her father. He wrote briefly that letters from home had urged him to come back; and that of course he could not leave without saying good-bye, and thanking them for having made his travels so pleasant. When he had despatched this note, he walked up and down restlessly until he received an answer. At last his messenger returned with a little three-cornered letter. Though the shape of the envelope had a suggestion of frivolity, the handwriting was large and clear and regular. She wrote that she was sorry that he was going, and doubly sorry that he was going so soon, because her father had gone to see the English fleet and would not be back in time to say good-bye; and then she named an hour at which she would be delighted to receive him. And that was all. As Dick stood twisting the note in his fingers, he thought it strange that she had not appended to her invitation some allusion to transatlantic customs and to his supposed British prejudice against calling on young ladies. If she had, he would have condemned it as bad taste; as it was, he said to himself bitterly, that her note was exactly what it ought to be. "A most accomplished young lady!" he said to

himself, as he began to tear the paper
across. Then he stopped, and put the note
back in its cover, and the cover into his
pocket; some day perhaps he would like to
have something to prevent him from entirely forgetting some interesting hours.

Dick walked about the streets till dinner-
time, and in spite of the inadequacy of the
world he came to the *table d'hôte* with a
fair appetite. There, as he was lucky
enough to sit next to a man whose conversation interested him, he almost forgot
his troubles for a time. His neighbour
was a Russian, and he was moreover that
rare creature, an educated Russian who
retained some enthusiasm. He spoke
English like a native, and as he found
that Dick listened with interest, he became eloquent in a quiet way on the
rotten condition of the Ottoman Empire,
on the impossibility of an Oriental state
in the civilised Europe of to-day, on its

barbarous customs, its incredible ignorance, the degradation of its women. Dick was inclined to agree with him that the life of Turkey in Europe could not be long; that the practical question was who was to be the successor. Upon this the Russian gentleman, with the greatest politeness, offered Dick Egypt in exchange for The Golden Horn; and though the young Englishman raised some objections on the ground of property, he found the suggestion interesting. Indeed their talk became lively; and it once or twice crossed Dick's mind how good a thing it was, that if one met with disappointments in private life, there were still the affairs of the nation, and that these at least were worthy of man's best efforts. He was so pleased with his conversation, that, when his new acquaintance suggested an adjournment after dinner to a neighbouring *café*, he agreed without hesitation.

This *café* in Pera had been established by Europeans for Europeans; and while the visitors smoked and drank, the stage at one end of the room was occupied by a company of French singers and comedians. At the moment when Dick entered, there was some applause and rapping of sticks on the tables, for a lady of the troupe was standing triumphant on one toe, while with her hand she clutched the high heel on her other foot high in air above her head. The strange thought came to the young Englishman that probably no dancing Dervish in the East could perform this agile feat. When this lithe lady's dance was done, another lady of ampler mould, with dead white skin and bold black eyes and a wide mouth full of uneven teeth, sang with a shrill metallic voice a little song full of Parisian slang and strange allusions. Then others sang and others danced; and yet in spite of all these efforts to amuse him,

somehow in the smoky air of the place
Dick's bitter mood crept back to him, and
he felt out of humour with life. He wondered if the Eastern barbarian, who wandered into this place of amusement, would
recognise the superiority of Western civilis-
ation, and the elevation of European women
above the degraded inmates of the Harem.
He remembered what he had heard in Syria
of the naturalised usurers, and how they
used the European consuls to extort their
monstrous interest; and he wondered if
this custom had impressed the Eastern mind
with the value of Western protection, and
the justice of Western rule. He wondered
if contemplation of the absolute trust and
open dealing, which prevailed between all
the civilised Governments of Europe, would
ever teach the Porte the value of a straightforward policy.

What would be the first step in progress? To turn the Mosque of St Sophia

into a church, or the gardens of the old Seraglio into a magnificent Cremorne ? Dick on that evening almost doubted the value of progress. He was heartily sick of the *café* and these accomplished Parisians—almost sick of life for the time being. As he walked home, he told himself that to improve the world was a dream like the rest. What a world it was, which he had thought so fair! Here girls played with hearts for their amusement; friend dared not stand by friend; reformers were mere Cavendish Tisleys; and a corrupt East was to be civilised forsooth by a corrupted West.

After a night less restful than the last Dick rose with the desire of flight twice as strong within him. If he seemed for the moment to have lost all other faith, he still believed that he could vanquish these bitter thoughts, which he could scarcely realise as his, when once he had

turned his back for ever on this ancient
city with its history of blood and crime.
He busied himself with getting everything
ready; but when there was no more to
be done, there was still an hour or more
before he could go to Miss Holcroft. He
walked about, and wished that the inter-
view was over; he told himself that it
could be nothing — nothing but a brief
visit of ceremony; he stopped himself again
and again from wondering what she would
say, or what she would think. It seemed
as if the time would never be gone; but
at last the hour had come, and he hurried
to say good-bye.

Miss Holcroft was alone, when Dick was
shown into the room. He had no eye for
details of costume; but yet he saw at a
glance that she was exquisitely, though
simply dressed; and the pains, which she
had taken to look her best, seemed to him
in his odd humour to put a final barrier

between them. He was conscious of a feeling of constraint which was new to him.
His manner was formal and chilly—prig-
gish, he supposed. He was so little used
to think about his manner, that thought
of it made him unlike himself. When
she had expressed regret at her father's
absence, and he had said something to
the same effect, there was a little pause,
and then she said—"I am so sorry you
are going away." She spoke in a tone
of kindness, and the words were kind ;
but to Dick in his unhappy mood they
seemed almost unmaidenly. If she were
sorry, he was sure that it was because flirtation is impossible without a man. He
thought that she might have let him go
without dressing herself up, and saying
soft things to him.

"It's time I went back," he said ; "there
are things to look after ; and they want me
to go in for politics."

Miss Holcroft made no comment on this information; she sat looking at him as if she expected him to talk. She had her back to the shaded light; and this made him uneasy, for he could not see the expression of her face. So he went on talking about politics and the state of parties in England, with a dreary indifference to both parties and to all politics.

"I wonder if you have any real reason for going," she said at last, when he seemed to have no more to say.

"Fifty," he said with an unnatural laugh. He felt that this should move her to prattle; when she said nothing, he was half angry with her silence; these pauses irritated him; he began asking about their plans, that she might be compelled to answer. But her answers were very short; for they seemed to have made no plans. She thought that they would not go home for at least a year; and that was all which she could tell him. He went on asking questions, and only half listening. The contrast of all this, which he was saying, with the words in his heart, made him feel like a mechanical doll.

At last he could stand it no longer; he rose to go. "I hope," he said, "that when you come to England, you will let me know; your father has my address; will you tell him? I should like to do something——"

He did not finish his sentence; she had risen too and was standing near him, but her face was still in shadow. She gave him her hand without a word; and he held it for a moment or two awkwardly. "Good-bye then," he said suddenly, as he dropped her hand from his. He went out and shut the door behind him; but in the instant before it was quite closed, he heard a sound, which made him stand still in the passage listening. He had shut the door behind him, before he had time to think that he had heard a sob. He stood still, but he heard nothing. He told himself that he had heard nothing. Anyway she was dramatic; that at least he knew; the proper end of such an episode, even of an episode so little sentimental as this, was of course a tear. He ran down-stairs and out into the street. A little later he was standing alone on the deck of the steamer, which moved slowly down the Bosphorus; he was already counting the days, which must pass, before he was again at home in England.

END OF THE SECOND VOLUME.

PRINTED BY WILLIAM BLACKWOOD AND SONS.